THE STREAMSIDE TERROR
vs.
THE HEMNOID AMBASSADOR

"You let him escape?" said the Terror, mildly.

"Alas," said Tark-ay, a trifle smugly.

"WHY?" roared the Terror. . . .

Note: noted John. Terror gives no warning. Does not telegraph punches. . .

Note: noted John. When no stream available, Terror attempts to batter opponent against handy rocks and trees. . .

Note: noted John. Liberal use of nails and teeth gives Terror considerable advantage over opponent not trained to this sort of fighting and not expecting same. . .

John suddenly realized that with all this noise going on, now was the ideal time for him to get away from the vicinity and travel.

He traveled.

Books by

GORDON DICKSON

ALIEN ART
ARCTURUS LANDING
PRO (Illustrated by James R. Odbert)
SPACIAL DELIVERY

from

ACE SCIENCE FICTION

SF

Spacial Delivery

GORDON R. DICKSON

SF
ace books
A Division of Charter Communications Inc.
A GROSSET & DUNLAP COMPANY
360 Park Avenue South
New York, New York 10010

SPACIAL DELIVERY

Copyright © 1961 by Ace Books, Inc.

An ACE Book

Cover art by Steve Hickman

This Ace printing: January 1979

Printed in U.S.A.

CHAPTER   1

THE Right Honorable Joshua Guy, Ambassador
Plenipotentiary to Dilbia, was smoking tobacco in a
pipe, an old-fashioned and villainous habit for such a
conservative and respected gentleman. The fumes
from the pipe made John Tardy cough and strangle.
Or perhaps it was the fumes combined with what the
Rt. Hon. Josh Guy had just said.

"Sir?" wheezed John Tardy.

"Sorry," said the dapper little diplomat. "Thought
you heard me the first time." He knocked his devil of
a pipe out in a hand-carved bowl of some native Dilbian wood, where the coal continued to smoulder and
stink only slightly less objectionably than it had
before. "What I said was that, naturally, as soon as
we knew you were safely drafted for the job, we let
out word to the Dilbians that you were deeply attached to the girl. In love with her, in fact."

John gulped air. Both men were talking Dilbian to
exercise the command of the language John had had
hypnoed into him on his way here from the Belt stars,
and the Dilbian nickname for the missing Earthian
girl sociologist came from his lips automatically,

"With this Greasy Face?"

"Miss Ty Lamorc," corrected Joshua, smoothly
slipping into Basic and then out again. "Greasy Face

to Dilbians, of course. But you mustn't pay too much attention to the apparent value of these Dilbian nicknames. The two old Dilbian gentlemen you're about to meet—Daddy Shaking Knees, Mayor of Humrog, here, by the way, and Two Answers—aren't at all the sort they might sound like from name alone. Daddy Shaking Knees got his name from holding up one end of a timber one day in an emergency. After about forty-five minutes someone noticed his knees starting to tremble a bit. And Two Answers is not a liar, as you might expect, but a wily sort who can come up with more than one solution to a problem."

"I see," said John.

"Miss Lamorc is quite a fine young women. I would not at all be ashamed to have her for a daughter, myself. Lots of character."

"Oh, I'm sure she has," said John, hastily. "I'm not objecting to the situation here. I don't want you to think that. After all, the draft is necessary in emergency situations, particularly in areas where we're in close competition with the Hemnoids. But I don't understand what this has to do with my decathlon record? I thought I'd put all that sports business behind me after the last Olympics. As you know, I'm actually a fully qualified biochemist, and . . ."

"Names," said Joshua, "have their chief value around here as an index to what the Dilbians think of you. I, myself, now, am referred to as Little Bite; and you will undoubtedly be christened yourself with a Dilbian nickname, shortly."

"Me?" said John, startled. He thought of his own red hair which surmounted an athletically stocky body. He had always hated to be called Red.

"It should not be too humiliating, provided you are

careful not to make yourself ridiculous. Heinie, now—"

"I beg your pardon?"

"I beg yours," said Josh, starting to refill his pipe. "I should have used his full name of Heiner Schlaff." He puffed fresh clouds of smoke into the air of the small, neat office with the log walls. "He lost his head first time he stepped out alone on the street. A Dilbian from one of the back-mountain clans who'd never seen a human before, picked him up. Heinie lost his head completely. After all, he was never able to poke his nose outdoors without some Dilbian picking him up to hear him yell for help. The Squeaking Squirt, they named him; very bad public relations for us humans. Particularly when Gulark-*ay*, the Hemnoid in charge of *their* embassy locally here, gets an advantageous handle hung on him like The Beer-Guts Bouncer. There he goes now, by the way."

Joshua pointed out the office window that fronted on the main street of Humrog. Coming down its cobblestones, John saw, a sort of enormous robed, Buddha-like parody of a human being. The Hemnoid was a good eight feet in height, enormously boned, and while not as tall as the Dilbians themselves, fantastically padded with heavy-gravity muscles. The Hemnoids, John remembered, came from an original world with one-fourth again the gravity of Earth. Since Dilbia's gravity was about a sixth less than Earth's, that gave humanity's chief and closest competitors quite an advantage in this particular instance.

"He may stop—no, he's going past," said Joshua. "What was I saying? Oh, yes. Keep your head in all situations. I assume someone who's won the decathlon in the All-Systems Olympics can do that."

"Well, yes," said John. "Of course, in biochemistry, now—"

"You will find the Dilbians primitive, touchy, and insular."

"I will?"

"Oh, yes. Definitely. Primitive. Touchy. And very much indifferent to anything outside their own mountains and forests; although we've been in touch with them for thirty years and the Hemnoids have for nearly twenty."

"I see. Well, I'll watch out for that," said John. "It struck me they wouldn't know much about chemistry, to say nothing of bio-chemistry—"

"On the other hand," Joshua brushed the neat ends of his small grey mustache with a thoughtful forefinger, "you mustn't fall into the error of thinking that just because they look like a passel of Kodiak bears who've decided to stand on their hind legs at all time and slim down a bit, that they're bearlike completely in nature."

"I'll watch that, too," said John.

"There are intelligent individuals among them. Highly intelligent. There's one," said Joshua, indicating a three-dimensional on his desk, the transparent cube of which showed the scaled-down frozen images of three Dilbians, the middle one of the trio—at whom Joshua was pointing—being a good head taller than either of his companions. Since John's hypno training had informed him that the average male adult Dilbian would scale upwards of nine feet, this made the one Joshua was pointing at a monster indeed. "He's shrewd. Independent and open-minded. Experienced and wise, to say nothing of being influential with his fellow-Dilbians. Is this pipe bothering you, my boy?"

"No. No," said John, coughing discreetly. "Not at all."

"Have to put it out shortly when we meet Daddy Shaking Knees and Two Answers. Dilbians are quite sensitive about human odors, even mild ones like tobacco. To get back to what I was saying: We *must* influence Dilbians like that chap or the Hemnoids are going to get the inside track on this planet. And the Dilbian system, as I'm sure your hypno training didn't omit to inform you, is absolutely necessary as a supply and reequipment stage for further expansion on any large scale beyond the Belt Stars. If the Hemnoids beat us out here, they've got the thin end of a wedge started that could eventually chop our heads off. Which they would be only too glad to do, you know."

John sighed. It was the sign of a very human, young, recent graduate in bio-chemistry who would have liked nothing better than to live and let live.

"You'd think there'd be room enough in the universe for both of us."

"Apparently not, in the Hemnoid lexicon. You must read up on their psychology sometime. Fascinating. They're actually less like us than the Dilbians are, in spite of their greater physical resemblance."

"I understand they can be pretty dangerous."

"They've an instinctive streak of cruelty. Do you know what they used to do to the elderly among their own people until just the last hundred years or so of their history—"

Beep, signaled the annuciator on Joshua's desk.

"Ah, that'll be Shaking Knees and Two Answers, in the outer office now," said the diplomat. "We'll go on in." He knocked out his pipe and laid it, regretfully, in the carved wooden bowl among the ashes.

"But what's it all about?" said John desperately. "I just got off the spaceship four hours ago. You've been feeding me lunch, and talking about background; but you haven't told me what it's all about!"

"Why, what's *what* all about?" asked Joshua, pausing halfway to the door to the outer office.

"Well—everything!" burst out John. "Why was I drafted? I was all set to trans-ship to McBanen's Planet to join my government exploration outfit, and this girl from the local embassy on Vega Seven where I was, came up and pulled my passport and said I was drafted to here. Nobody explained anything."

"Dear me! They didn't? And you just came along to Dilbia here by courier ship, without asking—"

"Well, I'm as good a citizen as anyone else," said John, defensively. "I mean I may not like the draft, but I realize the necessity for it. They said you needed me. I came. But I'd just like to know what it's all about before I start getting into the job."

"Of course, of course!" said Joshua. "Well, it's really nothing. Miss Lamorc, this young sociologist girl, the one I was talking about, got kidnapped, that's all. By a Dilbian. We want you to go bring her back. Old Shaking Knees in the next room is the father of Boy Is She Built. And it was the fact that the Streamside Terror wanted Boy is She Built that caused all this ruckus which ended up with the Terror kidnaping Miss Lamorc. You'll see," said Joshua, starting off toward the door again, "it's all very simple. It'll all straighten out for you once you get into it."

"But I don't see—" insisted John, doggedly, following him.

"What?" Joshua hesitated with his hand on the door latch.

"What all this has to do with my work. Why do you want a biochemist to bring back some woman who's been kidnapped?"

"But we don't particularly want a bio-chemist," said Joshua. "What we want is a rough, tough laddie with excellent physical reflexes of the kind that would take top honors in a decathlon competition. It isn't your brains we want, Mr. Tardy, it's your brawn." He opened the door. "You'll find it's all very simple once you get the hang of it. Come along, my dear boy. After you."

CHAPTER   2

POLITELY but firmly herded forward by the little diplomat, John found himself pushed into the large outer office of the Human Embassy on Dilbia, at Humrog, his head still spinning from Joshua's last words and the odd Dilbian names. Who, he wondered confusedly and in particular, was Boy Is She Built? The obvious conclusion, in terms of a seven foot-plus Dilbian female accoutered in little more than her natural furry pelt, was a little mind-shaking to imagine.

The moment, however, was not the proper one for imaginings, no matter how mind-shaking. Reality was being too overpowering to leave room for anything else. The first thing to strike John as the door closed behind him, was the scale of the room he was entering. The inner office had been a reassuringly human cell tucked away in a corner of gargantuan Dilbian architecture. Desk and chairs had been to John's own fit.

This outer office, for reasons of diplomatic politeness, was furnished in the outsize Dilbian scale. The heavy wall logs allowed for headroom up to fifteen feet below the log rafters. The bottom of the crudely glazed windows were on a level with John's chin. Several tables and straight-backed chairs fitted the rest of the furnishings by being of the same un-comfortable (by human standards) largeness. A quart-sized ink pot, and a hand-whittled pen holder about sixteen inches long on one of the tables, com-pleted the picture.

Not this, though, *nor* the hypno training, quite served to prepare John adequately for his first close-up encounter with a pair of the Dilbian natives. These two were standing not a dozen feet inside the door as John came through it; and their appearance assaulted his senses in all ways, immediately, and without warn-ing.

To begin with, they *smelled*. Not overpoweringly, not even unbearably, in fact rather like dogs that have been out in the rain for the first time in several weeks during which they have not had a bath. But, definite-ly, they smelled.

It did not help, either, for John to notice that the two were faintly wrinkling their large black noses at him, in turn.

And on top of this odor, there was the fact of the bigness of the room; which, after ten seconds, pulled a double switch on the senses; so that, instead of John feeling that he was the same size he had always been and the room was unnaturally big, the first thing he knew he was feeling that *it* was normal in dimensions and *he* had shrunk, all of a sudden, to the stature of a six-year old boy.

But last and not least was the center of all this, the two adult male Dilbians themselves, looking indeed like a pair of Kodiak bears who had stood up on their hind legs and gone on a diet. True, their brows were higher and more intelligent than bears. Their noses were shorter, their lower jaws more human-like than ursinoid. But their thick coats of brownish-black hair, their lumbering stance, massive shoulders and fore-arms and the fact that they wore nothing to speak of beyond a few leather straps and metal ornaments, shouted *bear* at you, any way you looked at it. If it was up to me, thought John. . . .

"Ah, there, Little Bite!" boomed the larger of the two furry monsters in native Dilbian, before he could finish the thought. "This the new one? Two Answers and I shook a leg right over here to give him the eye. Kind of bright colored up top there, ain't he?"

"Hor, hor, hor!" bellowed the other, thunderously. "Belt me, if I'd want one like him around. Liable to burn the house down! Hor, hor, hor!"

"Some of we humans have hair that color," replied Joshua. "Gentlemen, this is John Tardy. John, this gentleman with the sense of humor is Two Answers. And his quiet friend is Shaking Knees."

"Quiet!" roared the other Dilbian, exploding into gargantuan laughter. "Me, *quiet!* That's good!" He shook the heavy logs with his merriment.

John blinked. He glanced incredulously from the imperturbable Joshua to these oversize clowns in fur. What kind of goof-up, he wondered, could have put Guy in an ambassadorial post like this. A sharply tai-lored, fastidious little dandy of a man—and these loll-ing, shouting, belching, king-sized, frontier-type al-iens. It was past belief.

For the first time there crept into John's mind the awful suspicion that the whole thing—Joshua Guy being ambassador in a post like this, the kidnaping of the female sociologist, and his being drafted to do a job that he was in no way experienced or prepared for —all this was just part of one monstrous blunder that had its beginnings in the Alien Relations Office, back in Governmental Headquarters on Earth.

"Haven't laughed like that since old Souse Nose fell into the beer vat in the Mud Hollow Inn!" Two Answers was snorting, as he got himself back under control. "All right, Bright Top, what've you got to say for yourself? Think you can take the Streamside Terror with one paw tied behind your back?"

"I beg your pardon?" said John. "I understood I was here to bring back—er—Greasy Face, but—"

"Streamside won't just hand her over. Will he, Knees?" Two Answers jogged his companion with a massive elbow.

"Not that boy!" Shaking Knees shook his head, slowly. "Little Bite, I ought never have let you talk me out of a son-in-law like that. Tough. Rough. Tricky. My little girl'd do all right with a buck like that."

"I merely," said Joshua, "suggested you make them wait a bit, if you remember. Boy Is She Built is still rather young."

"And, boy is she built!" said her father, fondly. "Yep, I know it made sense the way you put it then." He shook his head a little. "You sure got the knack for coming up on the right side of the argument with a man. Still, now I look back on it, it's hard to see how that little girl of mine could do better." He peered suddenly at Joshua. "You sure you ain't got something hidden between your claws on this?"

Joshua spread his hands expressively.

"Would I risk one of my own people?" he said. "Maybe two, counting John, here? All for nothing but the fun of making the Terror mad at me?"

"Don't make sense, does it?" rumbled Shaking

Knees. "But you Shorties are tricky little characters." His words rang with an honest admiration.

"Now, you people are pretty sly yourselves," said Joshua. They both turned and spat over their left shoulders. "Well, now," went on Joshua, "compliments aside, anybody know where the Terror is?"

"He headed west through the Cold Mountains," put in Two Answers. "He was spotted yesterday a half day's hike north, pointed toward Sour Ford and the Hollows. He probably nighted at Brittle Rock Inn, there."

"Good," said Joshua. "We'll have to find a guide to there for my friend here."

"Guide? Ho!" chortled Shaking Knees. "Wait'll you see what we got for your friend." He shouldered past Two Answers, opened the door and bellowed. "Bluffer! In here!"

There was a moment's wait. And then a Dilbian even leaner and taller than Shaking Knees shouldered his way through the outer doorway into the office, which with this new addition, and in spite of its original size, began to take on the air of being decidedly crowded.

"Here you are, Shorties!" said Shaking Knees, waving an expansive furry hand at the newcomer. "What more could you ask for? Walk all day, climb all night, and start out fresh next morning after breakfast. Right, Hill Bluffer?"

"Right as rooftops in raintime!" sonorously proclaimed the newcomer, rattling the windows about the walls. "Hill Bluffer, that's my name and trade! Anything on two feet walk away from me? Not over solid ground or living rock! When I look at a hill, it knows it's beat; and it lays out flat for my trampling feet!"

"Well, how do you like that, Little Bite? Eh? How?" boomed Shaking Knees.

"Mighty impressive, Knees," replied Joshua. "But I don't know about my friend keeping up if the Hill Bluffer here moves like that."

"Keep up? Hah!" guffawed Shaking Knees. "No, no, Little Bite, don't you recognize the Hill Bluffer? He's the government postman from Humrog to Wildwood Peak. We're going to mail your Shorty friend here to the Terror. Guaranteed delivery. Postage: five pounds of nails."

"Nobody stops the mail." The Hill Bluffer swept the room with a glare that had a professional quality about it. "Nobody monkeys with the mail in transit!"

"Well. . . ." said Joshua, thoughtfully. "Five pounds, of course, is out of the question."

"Out of the question?" roared Shaking Knees. "A guaranteed, absolutely safe government mailman—!"

"I can hire five strong porters off the street for that."

"Sure you can. Sure!" jeered Shaking Knees. "But can any of them catch up with the Terror?"

"Can the Bluffer catch up?"

The Hill Bluffer bellowed like a struck bull.

"Well," said Joshua, "a pound and a half. That's fair."

The bargaining continued. John began to get a headache. He wondered how Joshua had kept from going deaf all these months in the embassy, or however long he had been billeted here. Then he noticed the older man was wearing a sound dampening coil behind each ear. It had not of course, thought John a trifle bitterly, occurred to him to suggest the same protection for John.

The price was finally settled at three and a quarter

pounds of steel nails, size and type to be at Shaking Knees' discretion, at some future date.

"Well, now," said Joshua, "the next thing is—how's the Bluffer going to carry him?"

"Who? Him?" boomed the Bluffer, focusing down on John. "Why, I'll handle him like he was a week-old pup. Wrap him up real careful in some soft straw, tuck him in the bottom of my mail pouch and—"

"Hey!" cried John.

"I'm afraid," said Joshua, "my friend's right. We're going to have to find some way he can ride more comfortably."

The meeting adjourned to the embassy warehouse adjoining, to see what could be rigged up in the way of a saddle.

"I won't wear it!" the Hill Bluffer was trumpeting, two hours later. They were all standing in the Humrog main street by this time, in front of the warehouse; and the cause of the Bluffer's upset, a system of straps and pads arranged into a sort of shoulder harness to carry John, lay on the cobblestones before them. A small number of local Dilbian bystanders had gathered; and their freely offered basso comments were not of a sort to bring the Hill Bluffer to a more reasonable frame of mind.

"Now, that's a real good system for my old lady to tote the youngest pup around," one Dilbian with a grey scar jaggedly across his black nose, was saying.

"Good training for the Bluffer, too," put in another blackfurred monster. "Have pups of his own, one of these days."

"Unless," said the scar-nosed one, judiciously, "this here little feller actually is a pup of the Hill Bluffer's, already."

"You don't mean to actually tell me!" said the other. He squinted at John. "Yep, there's a resemblance all right."

"You want your ear tore off," roared the infuriated Bluffer, pausing in the midst of his hot argument with Shaking Knees and Two Answers. "This here piece of mail's a Shorty!"

John backed off a little from the bellowing group and tried to shut the voices out of his mind, even if shutting them out of his ears was somewhat impractical. He was in that stage of helplessly worn-out exasperation which often results when naturally independent and strong-willed people are pushed around without explanation and without the chance for natural protest.

He turned his back on the shouting group and gazed off through the thin, clear air of the Dilbian mountains that made everything seem three times as close as they actually were, to a snow-laden peak thrusting up above the pinelike trees surrounding Humrog.

"At least try the unmentionable thing on!" Shaking Knees was roaring at the Hill Bluffer a dozen feet away.

Here, thought John, he had been hauled off the ship that was to take him out to his job with a government exploration team; it was work he had always wanted and just finished seven years of college-level study for. Instead he was on a citizen's draft which left him no chance to object. Well, yes, John had to admit to himself, the Draft Law provided he could refuse if he could charge the Drafting Authority—in this case, Joshua—with incompetence or misinformation. John snorted under his breath. Fine chance he had of doing that when he couldn't even find out what was going on. He had just stepped off his space-ship a few hours ago; and Joshua had yet to give him five minutes opportunity to formulate questions.

At the same time, thought John, there was some-thing awfully screwy about the way things were going on. As soon as this business of the saddle had been settled, he was going to haul Joshua aside, if need be by main force, and insist on some answers before he went any further. A citizen had some rights, too. . . .

"Arright, arright, arright!" snarled the Hill Bluffer barely six inches behind John's ear. "Buckle me up in the obscenity thing, then!"

John turned about to see Joshua pushing the sys-tem of straps up on the back of the Hill Bluffer, who was squatting down. Instinctively, he moved to give the little diplomat a hand.

"That's better!" growled Shaking Knees. "Don't blame you too much. But, you listen to me, pup! I happen to be your mother's uncle's first cousin, one generation up on you. And when I speak for a relative of mine of the second generation, he stays spoke for!"

"I'm doing it, ain't I?" flared the Bluffer. He wig-gled his shoulders experimentally. "Don't feel too bad at that."

"You'll find it," grunted Joshua, buckling a final strap, "easier to carry than your regular pouch."

"Not the point!" growled the Bluffer. "A postman's got dignity. He just don't wear—" a snicker from the scar-nosed Dilbian cut through his speech. *"Listen, you—Split Nose!"*

"I'll take care of him." Shaking Knees rolled for-ward a couple of paces. "What's wrong with you, Split Nose?"

"Just passing by," rumbled Split Nose, hastily

backing into the crowd as the Humrog village chief took a hand in the conversation.

"Well, then just pass on, friend. Pass on!" boomed Shaking Knees; and Split Nose trundled hastily off down the street with every indication his hairy ears were burning.

While this was going on, John, at Joshua's urging had seated himself in the saddle to see how it would bear his weight. The straps creaked, but held comfortably. The Hill Bluffer looked back over his shoulder.

"You're light enough," he said. "How is it? All right up there?"

"Fine," said John.

"Then, so long everybody!" boomed the Hill Bluffer.

He rose to his feet in one easy movement. And before John had time to do more than grab at the straps of the harness to keep from falling off, and catch his breath, they were barrelling off down the main street at the swift pace of the Bluffer's ground-eating stride, on their way to the forest trail, the mountains beyond which rose that distant peak John had just been watching, and the elusive and inimical Streamside Terror.

CHAPTER   3

IF IT had not been for the hypno training John had undergone, sitting with a large, bell-shaped helmet completely covering his head in the cramped little government scoutship, while on overdrive from the Belt Stars to Dilbia, he might instinctively have protested the Hill Bluffer's sudden departure. As it was, his pseudomemories of Dilbian life stood him in unexpectedly good stead. As it was, he had barely opened his mouth to yell, "Hey, wait a minute" when he suddenly 'remembered'. what consequences this might have and shut his lips firmly on the first syllable. As it was, the startled sound in his throat was enough to make the Hill Bluffer check his stride momentarily.

"Whazzat?" growled the Dilbian postman.

"Nothing," said John, hastily. "Clearing my throat."

"Thought you were going to say something," grunted the Bluffer, and swung back into his regular stride.

What John had suddenly 'remembered' was one of the little tricks possible under Dilbian custom. He, himself, had not expected to start out after the Lamorc girl until the next morning at the earliest; and then not without a full session with Joshua Guy in

18

which he would pin that elusive little man down about the whys and wherefores of the situation. As a citizen of the great human race it was his right to be fully briefed before being sent out on such a job.

That is, as a human citizen it was his right. As a piece of Dilbian mail, his rights were somewhat different—generally consisting of the postman's responsibility to deliver him without undue damage in transit to his destination.

Therefore, the little trickiness of the Hill Bluffer. As John had noticed, the postman had lost a great deal of his enthusiasm for the job on discovering the nature of the harness in which he would be carrying John. The Bluffer could not, of course, refuse to carry John without loss of honor, the hypno training informed John. But if a piece of mail should try to dictate the manner in which it was being delivered, then possibly Dilbian honor would stand excused, and the Bluffer could turn back, washing his hands of the whole matter.

So John said nothing.

All the same, he added another black mark to the score he was building up in the back of his mind against Joshua Guy. The Dilbian ambassador should have forseen this. John thought of the wrist phone he was wearing and began to compose a few of the statements he intended to make to that particular gentleman, as soon as he had a moment of privacy in which to make the call.

Meanwhile, the Bluffer went away down the slope of the main street of Humrog, turned right and began to climb the trail to the first ridge above the town. He had not been altogether exaggerating in his claims for himself as someone able to swing his feet. Almost immediately, it seemed to John, they were away from the great log buildings of the approximately five thousand population town of Humrog, and between the green thicknesses of the pinelike trees that covered the mountainous part of the rocky planet.

The Bluffer's long legs pistoned and swung in a steady rhythm, carrying himself and John up a good eight to ten degree slope at not much less than eight to ten miles an hour. John, swaying like a rider on the back of an elephant, concentrated on falling into the pattern of the Bluffer's movements and saving his own breath. The Bluffer, himself, said nothing.

They reached the top of the ridge and dipped down the slope into the first valley crossed by the trail. Long branches whipped past John as he clung to the Bluffer's shoulder straps and they plunged down the switchback trail as if any moment the Dilbian might miss his footing and go tumbling headlong off the trail and down the slope alongside.

Yet in spite of all this, John felt himself beginning to get used to the shifts of the big body under him. He was, in fact, responding with all the skill of an un-usually talented athlete already experienced in a number of physical skills. He was meeting in stride the problems posed by being a Dilbian-rider. In fact, he was becoming good at it, as he had always become good at such things—from jai alai to wrestling—ever since he was old enough to toddle beyond the con-fines of his crib.

Realizing this did not make him happy. It is a sort of inverse but universal law of nature that makes poets want to be soldiers of fortune, and soldiers of fortune secretly yearn to write poetry. John, a natu-rally born physical success, had always dreamed of the day his life could be exclusively devoted to peering through miscroscopes and writing scholarly reports. Fate, he reflected not without bitterness, was operating against him as usual.

"What?" demanded the Hill Bluffer.

"Did I say something?" asked John, starting guiltily back to the realities of his situation.

"You said *something*," replied the Hill Bluffer darkly. "I don't know what, exactly. Sounded like something in that Shorty talk of yours."

"Oh," said John.

"That's what I figured it was," said the Bluffer. "I mean, if it had been something in real words, I would have understood it. I figure any talking you'd be doing to me would be in regular speech. A man wouldn't want anyone making cracks behind his back in some kind of talk he couldn't understand."

"Oh, no. No," said John, hastily. "I was just sort of daydreaming—about things back on the Shorty world where I come from."

The Hill Bluffer absorbed this information in silence for a moment or two, during which he reached the bottom of one small valley and started up its far side.

"You mean," he said, after a moment, "you been *asleep* back there?"

"Uh—well—sort of dozing. . . ."

The Bluffer snorted like a small laboratory explosion and put on speed. He did not utter a word for the next two hours. Not, in fact, until someone beside John appeared on the verbal horizon to offer an excuse for conversation.

This new individual turned out to be another Dilbian, very much on the shaggy side, who appeared suddenly out of the woods on to the path ahead of them as they were crossing the low-slung curve of one of the interminable valleys. The stranger was carrying over one shoulder one of the local wild herbivores, a type of musk ox, large by human rather than Dilbian standards. In his other hand swung an ax with a seven foot handle.

The head of the ax was a thick, grey triangle of native iron, one leading side forming the edge of the blade, and the point at the far end being drawn back into a hook. A wicked-looking tool and weapon which John's hypno training now reminded him was carried and used on all occasions of civil and police matters.

But never used in brawls or combats. The Dilbians considered reliance on any weapon to be rather unmanly.

The Dilbian who had just appeared, waited agreeably in the path for them to catch up. John's nose, which was getting rather used to the Hill Bluffer by this time, discovered the newcomer's odor to be several notches more powerful than that of the Dilbians' he had met so far. This Dilbian also had a couple of teeth missing and was plentifully matted about the shoulder and chest with blood from the dead animal he was carrying. He grinned in gap-toothed interest at John; but spoke to the Bluffer, as the Bluffer stopped before him.

"Bluffer," he said.

"Hello, woodsman," said the Bluffer.

"Hello, postman." The gap-toothed grin widened. "Anything for me in the mail?"

"You!" The Bluffer's snort rang through the woods.

"Not so funny!" growled the other. "My second cousin got a piece of mail, once. His clan was gathering at Two Falls; he was a Two Faller through his mother's blood aunt . . ." the woodsman went on heatedly in an apparent attempt to prove his cousin's genealogical claim to have received the piece of mail in question.

Meanwhile, John's attention had been attracted by something else back in the trees from which the woodsman had just emerged. He was trying to get a clearer view of it without betraying himself by turning to look directly at it. It was hard to make out there in the deep shadow behind the branches of the trees, but there seemed to be two other individuals standing back out of sight and listening.

Neither one was a human being. One seemed to be a Dilbian, a small, rather fat-looking Dilbian. And the other, John was just about prepared to swear, was a Buddha-like Hemnoid. It was infuriating that just as he was about to get a clear glimpse of this second individual, a breeze or movement of the air would sway a branch in the way of his vision. If it were a Hemnoid. . . .

John's hypno training, possibly by reason of the general snafu that seemed to effect anything having to do with John and Dilbia in general, had omitted to inform him about the Hemnoids. Accordingly, all he knew about this race, which were neck-and-necking it with the humans in a general race to the stars, was what he had picked up in the ordinary way through newspapers and chance encounters.

The Hemnoids looked exactly like jolly fat men half again the size of a human. Only what looked like fat was mostly muscle resulting from a heavier-than-earth gravity on their home world. And they were not

—repeat, not—jolly, in the human sense of the word. They had a sense of humor, all right; but it was of the variety that goes with pulling wings off flies. John's only personal encounter with a Hemnoid before this had been at the Interplanetary Olympiad in Brisbane, Australia, the year John had won the decathlon competition.

The Hemnoid ambassador, who had been in the stands that day to witness the competition, came down afterwards to be introduced to some of the athletes; he amused himself by putting the shot two hundred and twenty feet, making a standing broad jump of twenty-eight feet, and otherwise showing up the winners of the recent events. He had then laughed uproariously and suggested a heavy-fat diet such as he followed himself, and also hard physical labor.

If he had time, he said, he would be glad to train a school of athletes who would undoubtedly sweep the next Olympics. Alas, he had to get back to his embassy in Geneva. But let them follow his advice, which would undoubtedly do wonders for them. He had then departed, still chuckling.

While over by the sawdust pit of the pole vault, half the Italian track team were engaged in restraining one of their number, the miler Rudi Maltetti, who had gotten his hands on a javelin and was threatening to cause an interstellar incident.

"So that's the Half-Pint Posted."

John came back to the present with a start, suddenly realizing that the words the woodsman had just spoken were in reference to himself. He turned and stared over the Bluffer's shoulder at the other Dilbian, who was grinning at him in almost Hemnoid fashion. John had, it seemed, already been nicknamed as Joshua had predicted.

"What do you know about him?" the Bluffer was demanding.

"The Cobbly Queen told me," said the other, curling up the right side of his upper lip in the native equivalent of a wink. John recalled that the Cobblies were the Dilbian equivalents of elves, brownies, or what-have-you. He wondered if the woodsman could be serious. John decided the Dilbian wasn't, which still left the problem of how he had recognized John.

"Who're you?" demanded John, taking advantage of the best Dilbian manners, which allowed anybody to horn in on any conversation.

"So it talks does it?" said the woodsman. The Hill Bluffer snorted and threw a displeased glance over his own shoulder. "They calls me Tree Weeper, Half-Pint. Becuase I chops them down, you see."

"Who told you about me?"

"Ah, that's telling too much," grinned the Tree Weeper. "Call it the Cobbly Queen and you've half of it, anyway. You knows why they call him the Streamside Terror, don't you, Half-Pint? It's because he likes to do his fighting alongside a stream, and pull the other man in the water and get him drowned."

"Oh?" said John. "I mean—sure, I know that."

"Does you now?" said the other. "Well, it ought to be something to watch. Good luck, Half-Pint then; and you, too, road walker. Me for home and something to eat."

He turned away; and as he did so, John got a sudden glimpse past him in between the trees at the two who waited back in the shadow. The Dilbian he did not identify; but the Hemnoid was a shorter, broader individual than Gulark-ay, one who evidently had his nose broken at one time or another. Then, the Hill Bluffer started up again with a jerk. John lost sight of the watchers.

The Tree Weeper had stepped in among the brush and trees on the far side of the road and was immediately out of sight. A few final sounds marked his going—it was surprising how quietly a Dilbian could move if he wanted to—and then they were out of hearing. The Hill Bluffer swung anew along his route without a word.

John was left sorting over what he had just discovered. He searched his Dilbian 'memories' for the proper remark to jolt the Hill Bluffer into conversation.

"Friend of yours?" he inquired.

The Hill Bluffer snorted so hard it jolted John in his saddle.

"Friend!" he exploded. "A backwoods tree-chopper? I'm a public official, Half-Pint. You remember that."

"I just thought—" said John, peaceably. "He seemed to know a lot about me, and what was going on. I mean, about the Streamside Terror and the fact we're after him. But nobody's passed us up—"

"Nobody passes me up," said the Bluffer, bristling apparently automatically.

"Then, how—"

"Somebody leaving just ahead of us must've told him!" growled the Bluffer.

But he fell unaccountably silent after that, so that John could get nothing further out of him. And the silence lasted until, finally, they pulled up in the late afternoon sunlight before the roadside inn at Brittle Rock, where they would stay the night.

CHAPTER 4

THE first thing John did on being free once more of his saddle was to take a stroll about the area of the inn to stretch the cramps out of his legs. He was more than a little bit unsteady on his feet. Five hours on top of a hitherto unknown mount is not to be recommended even for a natural athlete. John's thighs ached, and his knees had a tendency to give unexpectedly, as if he had spent the afternoon climbing ladders. However, as he walked, more and more of his natural resilience seemed to flow back into him.

Brittle Rock Inn and grounds constituted, literally, a wide spot in the mountain road which John and the Hill Bluffer had been traveling. On one side of the road was a rocky cliff face going back and up at something like an eighty degree angle. On the other side was a sort of flat, gravelly bulge on the kind that would make a scenic highway parking spot in the mountain highways back on Earth. On this bulge was situated the long, low shape of the inn, built of untrimmed logs. Behind the inn was a sort of trash and outhouse area stretching about twenty yards or so to the edge of a rather breathtaking dropoff into a canyon where a mountain river stampeded along, pell-mell, some five hundred feet below. A picturesque spot, for those in the mood for such.

John was not in the mood. As soon as his legs began to feel less like sections of rubber tire casings and more like honest flesh and bone, he walked up along the bulge toward the spot where it narrowed into a road, again. Here, in relative isolation, he called Joshua on his wrist phone.

The ambassador responded at once. He must, thought John, have been wearing a wrist phone himself.

"Hello? Hello!" said Joshua's voice tinnily from the tiny speaker of John's wrist phone. "John?"

"Yes, sir," said John.

"Well, well! How are you?"

"Fine, thanks," said John. "How are you?"

"Excellent. Excellent. But I suppose you had some reason for calling?"

"I'm at Brittle Rock," said John. "We just got here. We're going to stay the night. Can you talk freely?"

"Talk freely? Of course I can talk freely, why shouldn't I?" The wrist phone broke off suddenly on a short barking laugh. "Oh, I see what you mean. No, I was just having a drink before dinner, here. Quite alone. What did you want to say?"

"Why, I thought you might have some instructions for me," said John. "The Hill Bluffer ran off with me back at Humrog before you really had a chance to brief me. I thought you could tell me now."

"Tell you?" said the phone. "But my dear boy! There's nothing to tell. You're to run down the Streamside Terror and bring back Miss Ty Lamorc. What else do you need to know?"

"But—" began John, and stopped. He did not know what he needed to know; he merely felt the need of a large area of necessary knowledge like a general ache or pain. At a loss to put this effectively into words, he was reduced to staring at his wrist phone.

"No sign of the Terror, yet?" inquired the phone, politely filling in the gap in the conversation.

"No."

"Well, it'll probably take several days to catch up with him. Just feel your way as you go. Things will undoubtedly work out. Follow your nose. Play it by ear. Otherwise, just relax and enjoy yourself. Beautiful scenery up there around Brittle Rock, isn't it?"

"Yes," said John numbly.

"Yes, I always thought so, myself. Well I'll ring off, then. Call me any time you think you might need my help. Good-by."

The voice in the phone broke the connection with a click. John shut off the power source at his end. A little sourly, he headed back toward the inn. It was against all known rules of biology, but he wondered if Joshua might not be part Hemnoid, from one of the sides of his family.

The mountain twilight had been dwindling as he talked; but his eyes had automatically adjusted to the failing light so that it was not until he stepped in through the hide curtain that protected the front entrance to the inn, that he realized how dark outside it had become. The thick, flaring candles around the room, the smells and the noise within struck him as he entered, leaving him for a moment half-stunned and blinded.

The ordinary Dilbian inn, his hypno 'memories' told him, was divided into a common room, a dormitory, and a kitchen. He had just stepped into the common room of this one; and he found it a

square crowded space, jammed with wooden benches
and tables like picnic tables at which three or four
Dilbians could sit at once. There were about twenty
or so Dilbians seated around it, all of them drinking
and most of them arguing. The Hill Bluffer, he discovered, was off to one side arguing with a female
Dilbian wearing an apron.

"But can't you tell me what to feed it?" the innkeeperess or whatever she was, was demanding,
wringing her oversized, pawlike hands.

"Food!" roared the Hill Bluffer.

"But what kind of food? You haven't had the children dragging in one pet after another, like I have. I
know. You feed it the wrong thing, and it dies. You're
going to have to tell me exactly what—"

"How the unmentionable should I know exactly
what?" bellowed the Bluffer, waving his arms furiously in the air and vastly entertaining those other guests
of the inn who were nearby. "Give him something.
Anything. See if he eats it. Some meat, some beer.
Anything!"

"Talking about me?" inquired John.

They all looked down, discovering his presence for
the first time. "Where'd he come from?" several of
them could be heard inquiring audibly; although
John had practically stepped on their toes on the way
in.

"It talks!" gasped the innkeeperess.

"Didn't I say he did?" demanded the Bluffer.
"Half-Pint, tell her what you want to eat."

John fingered the four-inch tubes of food concen-
trate clipped to his belt. Joshua had handed them to
him in a rather off-hand fashion that very morning;
but with no suggestion that he might be shortly using

them. Apparently there had been something more than coincidence at work, however. John's hypno training reminded him now that while Dilbian food would nourish him, it might also very well trigger off some galloping allergy. He was not, at the present moment, in the mood for hives, or a case of eczema. The tubes would have to do. With something for bulk.

"Just a little beer," he said.

He could sense the roomful of Dilbians around him warming to him, immediately. Beer-drinking was a man's occupation. This small, alien critter could not be, they seemed to feel, *too* alien if he enjoyed a good drink.

The innkeeperess went off to fill John's order and John climbed up on one of the benches, put his elbows on the table and found himself more or less in the position of a five-year-old on Earth whose chin barely clears the parental tabletop. The beer arrived in a wooden, foot and a half high mug that smelled as sour as the most decayed of back-lot breweries. There was no handle. John looked about him.

The others in the room were all sitting, Dilbian polite fashion, with one furry leg tucked underneath them, watching him, and waiting. John pulled his right leg up under his left, seized the mug in both hands, tilted its top-heavy weight, and gulped. A bitter, sour, flat-tasting liquid flowed down his throat. He swallowed, hastily, suppressing an urge to sputter, and set the mug back down, wiping his lips appreciatively with the back of his hand.

The room buzzed approval. And returned to its regular business.

John, left alone, swallowed a couple of times, finding the aftertaste not so bad as he had feared. Beer, in the sense of a mildly alcoholic beverage brewed from a fermented cereal, is after all, beer. No matter where you find it; and now that the first shock was over, John's taste buds were discovering similarities between this and other liquids of a like nature that they had encountered aforetime.

John surreptitiously uncrooked his leg, which was beginning to cramp, and turned to the Hill Bluffer to ask whether there had been any word of the Streamside Terror having passed, or news or his captive. But the Dilbian postman had disappeared.

Thoughtfully, John took another, and smaller, drink from his mug absentmindedly noting that this one was not so bad. It occurred to him that the Hill Bluffer might just have stepped out somewhere for a moment. In any case, John himself would be safer to stick where he was than go incautiously running around among the guests, most of whom had already finished eating and settled down to a serious evening of drinking.

But the Hill Bluffer did not return. John found his mug was empty. A few minutes later the innkeeperess replaced it with a full one, whether on the Bluffer's orders, or her own initiative, John did not know. John was rather surprised to find he had drunk so much. He was not ordinarily a heavy drinker. But it was hard not to take large gulps from the clumsy and heavy mug; and it was hard to take human-sized swallows when all around him Dilbians were taking a half-pint at a sip, so to speak.

The common room, John decided, was after all, a rough, but friendly place. The Dilbians were good sorts. What had ever given him the idea that wander-

ing around among them might not be safe? It occurred to him abruptly that it might be a clever move
to go find the Bluffer. Bring the postman back to the
table here. Buy him a beer and under the guise of casual conversation find out how the Dilbians really felt
on the human-versus-Hemnoid question. John
slipped down from the bench and headed off toward
the inner door through which the innkeeperess had
just disappeared.

The door, like the one outside, had a hide curtain.
Pushing the heavy mass of this aside, John found
himself in a long room, halfway down the side of
which ran an open stone trough in which charcoal
was burning. A rude hood above this ran to a
chimney that sucked out most of the smoke and
fumes to the quick overhead whip of the constant
mountain winds.

Various Dilbians of all ages, mostly female or
young, he noted, were moving around the fires in the
trough and a long table that paralleled it, running
down the room's center. Produce and carcasses hung
from the wooden ceiling rafters and kegs were racked
up near the back entrance of the kitchen. He recognized the innkeeperess through the steam and smoke,
busy filling a double handful of mugs from one of the
kegs; but the Bluffer was nowhere in the room. Those
who were, ignored him as completely as had the spectators in the common room earlier, before he had
spoken up. He waited until the innkeeperess was done
and headed toward her. Then he stepped directly into
her path.

"Eeeek!" she said, or the Dilbian equivalent, as she
recognized him. She stopped dead, spilling some of
the beer. "What are you doing in here? Get out!" She

looked at him, uncertainly. "That's a good little Shorty," she said, changing the tone of her voice. "Go back to your nice table, now."

"I was looking for the Hill Bluffer—" began John.

"Bluffer's not here. Now, you go back to your table. Is your mug all empty? I'll bring you some more in just a minute."

"Just a second. As long as I've got you," said John, "can you tell me if the Streamside Terror came through here yesterday? He'd have had a Shorty like myself along. Did they stay here for the night?"

"He just stopped in for some meat and beer. I didn't see any Shorty," said the innkeeperess, a hint of impatience creeping into her tone. "In fact, I didn't see him. Wouldn't have cared if I did. I've no time for hill-and-alley brawlers. Fight, fight, that's all they think of! When's the work to get done? Now, shoo! Shoo!"

John shooed, back toward his table. The Hill Bluffer was still among the missing in the common room; but as John was climbing with a certain amount of effort back up onto his bench, he felt himself seized from behind and lifted into the air. Craning his head back to look over his shoulder, he saw he was being carried by a large male Dilbian with a pronounced body odor reminiscent of the woodchoppers, and a large pouch slung from one shoulder. This Dilbian seemed rather more than a little drunk.

Whooping cheerfully, the Dilbian staggered across the room, carrying John and came bang up against another table where two more villainous-looking characters like himself were sitting.

CHAPTER 5

JOHN found himself dropped on top of the table between them, as the Dilbian who had brought him over thumped down heavily on a bench behind John. Instinctively, John scrambled to his feet. He found himself surrounded by three large, furry faces in a circle about three feet in diameter. One of the faces had halitosis.

"There he be," said the one who had brought John over. "A genuine Shorty."

"Full-growed, do you think?" inquired one of the others, a Dilbian with a broken nose and a scar creasing the fur of his face. It was the third one at the table, evidently, who needed to brush his teeth.

"Sure, he is," said the drunken one, indignantly. "You don't think they'd let him run around here unless he was all the way grown up?"

"Give him some beer," interjected the halitosis one, hoarsely.

A mug was thrust at John, who in prudence took it and tilted it to his mouth.

"Don't drink much," said Halitosis, after John had set the mug down, his already somewhat alcoholized head swimming after what had actually been a healthy human-sized draft of the liquid. "Like a bird. Like a little bird."

35

"Built man-shape, though," commented the one with the broken nose. "I wonder if he. . . ." The question was of purely physiological significance.

"Not likely, at that size," said the drunken one. "Hear he's chasing this here Shorty female the Terror's got, though. You reckon. . . .?"

One of the others—it was Halitosis again—hoarsely regretted the fact that they did not have the Shorty female there as well. It would, in his opinion, provide an opportunity for interesting and educative experimentation.

"Go to hell!" said John, instinctively in Basic Human.

"What?" asked the one with the pouch, drunkenly, behind him.

John made the most forceful translation into Dilbian that he could manage. The three Dilbians exploded into laughter.

"Have another drink," said Broken Nose; and a further pint or so of the beer was forced down John's throat. Broken Nose turned to his friends. "He better not get too tough with me, though!" He made a few humorous swipes with one huge hand in the air over John's head. John felt his hair fanned by the blows, which would have had little trouble splitting his skull wide open if they had connected.

Everybody laughed.

"I wonder, can he do tricks?" asked Halitosis.

"How about it, Shorty?" demanded the drunken Dilbian with the pouch, who seemed to have adopted an air of ownership toward John.

"Sure," said John.

"Show 'em one!"

"Give me a full mug of beer, then," said John. The

three contributed from other mugs until one was brimming full—amongst guesses, polite and impolite —as to what the trick might require the beer for. When the mug was full, John reached down and hefted the gallon and a half container in his arms, taking a good grip on it.

"Now, watch closely," he said. "I take a firm hold here, rock back on my heels like this, and—"

He spun suddenly on one heel, swinging the mug around and sloshing a wave of beer into all three faces. As they ducked and pawed at their eyes, he leaped the table, dodged under the nearest bench, and continued in a sort of broken-field run for the door. At any minute, he expected a large hand to reach down and capture him; but although he found himself forced to give opportunities for this, no one else seemed inclined to halt him. The rest of the common room of the inn was roaring with laughter at the three belonging to the table he had just left. And these were cursing, rooting around and overturning nearby benches under the evident impression that John was still in their immediate area. The door to the outside loomed before John. He ducked gratefully under its hide curtain and into the safety of the outer darkness.

He did not immediately halt on gaining the security of the night, but continued around the side of the inn toward the bare patch of trashyard behind it that stood between the inn and the dropoff into the gorge, down in which he could hear the unseen mountain river even now, brawling on its nighttime way.

He wanted room. Once behind the inn, he dropped into a sitting position in the shelter of some empty kegs that, with other junk, filled the area. Off to his right, a rectangle of light framed the hide curtain covering a door to the inn. From that door came the odors of cooking and the sound of quarreling voices. A back kitchen entrance, apparently.

John sat, breathing heavily and trying to pull himself together. To his annoyance, he was more than a little drunk. The quart or so that the three at the table had forced him to drunk on top of what he had already had, was now piling up inside him to give him a noticeable fuzziness. It would not last too long since it was the result of fast, rather than heavy, drinking. But for the moment it put him at a definite disadvantage in any contest where his only defense against overwhelming size and strength would be his natural speed and alertness. He decided to sit still where he was until his head was clear again, even if that took a couple of hours or so. Then carefully reconnoiter the place for the Hill Bluffer, in whose shadow he could enjoy some security.

He had just made up his mind to this, and was beginning to get his breath back, when there was a sudden flash of light from the hide curtain. Looking up, he caught sight for a moment of a female Dilbian figure, a small one, framed in silhouette for a second against the glare within. Then, swiftly, the curtain fell back into place, leaving only its pencil outline of yellow illumination.

But John had a sudden, uncomfortable feeling that the female he had seen had remained outside, rather than within. Quickly and quietly, he got to his feet in the darkness.

No sound from the direction of the door reached his ears; but he remembered how quietly the Tree Weeper had gone off through the woods as he left John and the Bluffer. And there had been no reason for the woodsman to hide the noise of his passage. If that was any index, and the Dilbian he had seen in the doorway was actually out here hunting him for any reason, John would have to rely on more than his ears for warning of any approach.

He lifted his nose and sniffed, cautiously. The kitchen odors had pretty much taken charge of the night air, but . . . yes, he was sure he caught a whiff of the peculiar Dilbian body odor.

And just at that moment, not ten feet from him, he heard clearly the sound of a double sniff.

Mentally kicking himself for his stupidity in forgetting that where human and Dilbian were concerned, two could play at this nose game, John moved speedily and silently away from the spot where he had been resting. The thing to do now, he thought, was to get upwind of his hunter, or huntress—if indeed it was the small female he had seen silhouetted, and then try to dodge past and get around once more to the front of the inn. Even Halitosis and his friends would be safer company than he was enjoying out here.

John began to move cautiously around to his right, toward the unseen and sounding river below the edge of the dropoff. No noise followed him; and this silence by itself was disturbing. John breathed shallowly and quietly, straining his eyes against the obsidian dark. He thought he saw something moving—black against black—but he was not sure. With the utmost possible silence, he began to back away, crouching. If he could find the edge of the cliff without falling over it, and work back along to a point level with the end of the inn, perhaps a quick dash from that spot for the inn's front door—

The odds were against him. Just at that moment, he

tripped and fell over a broken hoop from a keg.

The thud and clatter of his fall cried out in the tense silence. There was a sudden, tearing rush at him by something large and invisible; he rolled frantically free, stood up and ran.

There was no moon showing over this part of Dilbia in this season of the year, and the starlight gave little illumination. Still, what there was was enough to show him the ragged edge of the dropoff. He skidded to a halt, just short of tumbling headlong into the canyon. He stopped and turned, half-crouched, holding his breath and listening.

His heart hammered. There was no other sound.

End of round one, his brain suggested idiotically. And beginning of round two. Seconds out of the corners.

He held his breath and went on listening. For a long minute or two he heard nothing. Then, at some short distance behind him, he heard again the faint but unmistakable sound of sniffing. He froze. He was between the wind blowing up over the edge of the dropoff, and whoever hunted him. That sniffing nose would lead the pursuer straight to him.

Step by step, like a cat cautiously crossing a basket of eggs, he began to back up along the lip of the cliff. He had been blocked off from escape around the near end of the inn. Possibly he could retreat and make another try, this time around the far end. That is, if the hunter didn't catch up with him before he got that far, as was more than likely.

John took a moment now to wish that he had picked up a piece of barrel hoop, or some sort of a weapon from the trash lying about the yard. The female he had seen framed in the doorway was not so

much bigger than he that something in the way of a
club might not give him a fighting chance. He
stretched out his hands as he went, sweeping the
ground, in hopes of encountering something that
could be put to use defensively.

His fingers trailed over the stones of the ground;
then touched something hard, but a moment's feeling
about showed it to be the end of a complete keg, and
useless for his purposes. A little farther, he encountered a barrel hoop, but it was complete and roundly
harmless. It was not until the third try, that he found
something useful.

It was a chunk of what was probably kindling
wood to one Dilbian size, a length of split, dried log
about four inches thick and about two and a half feet
long. It was better than nothing and John's hand
closed gratefully about it, taking it with him.

He was three-quarters of the way to the far end of
the inn, now. A little farther, and perhaps he would
not need the chunk of kindling after all. A little
farther. . . .

He had backed clear to a point level with the end of
the inn, and its front side was less than thirty yards
away. One quick dash and he would be safe. John
froze and sniffed silently. He listened.

Silence held the night.

John turned his head slowly from right to left, scan-
ning the darkness behind him and the darkness between him and the inn. Over the rushing of the waters
far below he could hear, through the bones of his inner ear, the creak of his tense neck muscles moving in
the ringing silence of the waiting hush.

Nothing could be seen. Nothing moved. End of
round three, whispered his brain. Beginning of round

four. Seconds out of their corners. Still holding the club, he got up on his toes and knuckles like a sprinter about to start.

There was a sudden movement. A rearing up in the darkness before him. He tried to dodge, felt his feet slipping in the loose gravel and rock, struck out with the club and felt it connect. . . .

And something indescribably hard smashed down onto his head, sending him swirling down and away, into starshot blackness.

CHAPTER 6

JOHN opened his eyes to bright sunlight.

Dilbia's sun, just above the snow-gilt peaks of the mountain horizon, was shining its first clear rays of the day directly into his eyes. He blinked sleepily, and started to roll over onto his side, turning his back to the penetrating dazzle of the light—

—and grabbed with every ounce of strength he could summon at the rough trunk of a stubby tree growing sideways out of the granite rock beside him.

For a long second, he hung there sweating. Then he wriggled back a ways, but without releasing his grip on the little tree, until he felt himself firmly wedged in among the rocks around him. Then—but still not letting go on the tree—he risked another look.

He lay on a narrow ledge several hundred feet above a mountain river and eternity. The water was far below. How far, he did not take the time or trouble to estimate. It was far enough.

He turned over and looked up. Just above him, a slight overhang came to an end, then there was about fifteen feet of jagged rock cliffside, then a steep slope, and some small sweaty distance beyond that, the haven that was the edge of the inn's backyard. A bit of rusty hoop overhanging the edge identified it as such.

Swallowing a little convulsively, John relaxed his grip on the tree.

He was wide awake now, and in condition to notice a number of scrapes and gouges. There was one plowed groove that started up from his wrist and almost made it to his elbow. For a second John almost regretted not being back comfortably asleep again. Then he remembered the gorge below and was glad he was not. He looked up at the cliff face above him once more, and began to pick out a route by which he could ascend it.

He found it easily enough. The climb was not one which called for mountaineering experience, though John had that, along with other sports qualifications. But, thought John as he climbed, it was not exactly what everybody would pick for exercise before breakfast.

He made it up over the lip of the yard and lay there for a second, panting. In the daylight, the yard looked very small and ordinary. It was hard to believe that it had been the lengthy and dangerous arena where he had skulked and fought for his life the night before. John got to his feet, brushed himself off, and limped around to the front of the inn, where some commotion seemed to be in process, and stumbled upon a scene that made him blink.

The entire populace of the inn, guests and help alike, were drawn up in the road before it. They stood in fairly orderly ranks before an open space in which a grizzled and lean old Dilbian sat on a bench placed on top of a table. Between this individual and the crowd—among which John recognized the innkeeperess in a clean apron—were John's three tormentors of the night before, looking hangdog between two large Dilbians carrying axes over their shoulders. What, from its stained and gouged appearance looked ominously like a chopping block, was in position a little in front of the prisoners.

Across from the prisoners, the Hill Bluffer was windmilling his arms and orating in a tone of outrage.

"The mail!" he was roaring, as John tottered around the corner of the inn into the full sight of everybody. "The mail is sacred. Anyone laying hands upon the mail in transit—"

At that moment, he caught sight of John; and broke off. The total assemblage, including the judge, turned and stared at John as he limped forward into their midst.

"There!" burst out the innkeeperess. "Didn't I say it? The poor little fellow—probably frightened out of his wits. Been up a tree all this time, no doubt. No reason at all for chopping three poor men who're just having a friendly drink. But, that's it for you, a man can't get beyond his middle years but he has to be playing judge at every opportunity. And every man who ever wore a mail pouch ranting and raving as if there wasn't anything in the world but letters—much good letters do anyone, anyway. And those who can't wait to waste their good time standing around at a trial and an execution not much better. Poor little Shorty." She swooped down on John, fluttering her apron at him. "Now you just get right inside there and have your morning beer. *Men!*"

John let himself be herded inside. In addition to all his other aches and pains, he had just discovered himself to be the possessor of a walking hangover. And the Dilbian beer was at present the quickest— and only—cure for that.

Later, after John had drunk his breakfast and washed off a certain amount of dried blood, he and the Hill Bluffer got under way again. The long-legged Dilbian had fizzed and popped with the effervescence of throttled outrage for the first fifteen minutes or so following John's return. But on being shut up by the innkeeperess, he had lapsed into a thoughtful silence, and he continued to be silent during the first few hours of their trip.

Meanwhile, thanks to a generally good physical condition and possibly in some measure to the beer and the food concentrates, John was recovering rapidly. Their way from Brittle Rock led through the highlands toward Knobby Gorge, the Bluffer had informed John, earlier. After that they would begin the gradual descent down the far, forested side of the Cold Mountains to Sour Ford and the Hollows. The Hollows was clan-country for the Streamside Terror, and their hope was to catch up with him before he reached it.

The first part of the day's trailing after they left Brittle Rock led by narrow mountainside paths and across swinging suspension bridges over deep cuts in the rock that ended, far below, in rushing currents of white water. The Hill Bluffer trod this way for the first couple of hours, not merely with the casualness of someone well-used to it, but with the actual absent-mindedness of a person in deep thought.

"Hey!" said John, finally, when for the fifth time that morning the Hill Bluffer had shown signs of intending to walk off the path on to several hundred feet of thin air.

"Huh? What?" grunted the Hill Bluffer, saving them both with a practised twist of an ankle. "What's that? Something on your mind, Half-Pint?"

As a matter of fact, thought John, there was. The notion born out of the fumes of the beer the previous evening when he had sat in what he thought was momentary safety in the inn's backyard—before whoever it was had come out the kitchen door to hunt him —had returned to mind this morning as not a bad idea after all. Why not, he thought again, find out an honest Dilbian point of view about the human-Hemnoid struggle to make friends with the natives of this world? It was something that might not only rate him a commendation after all this was over; but might furnish him some valuable pointers on his present situation. These first two hours of no conversation had given him a chance to turn the matter over in his mind and try to think of how to frame the question.

He had finally come to the conclusion that, considering the Dilbian character, a direct approach was probably the best.

"Yes," he said to the Hill Bluffer now. "I've been trying to figure out why you Dilbians like the Hemnoids better than us Shorties."

The Bluffer did not rise to the bait, as John had half-hoped by immediately denying that the Dilbians played favorites.

"Oh, that," said the Hill Bluffer, as calmly as if they were talking about a law of nature. "Why, it stands to reason, Half-Pint. Take the Beer-Guts Bouncer, now; or that new little one—"

"What new little one?" asked John, sharply, remembering the Hemnoid back in the woods when they had stopped to talk to Tree Weeper.

"What's his name—Tark-ay, I guess they call him. The one who's supposed to have been quite a scrap-

per back on his own home territory. You take someone like him, for example."

"What about him?" asked John.

"Well, now," said the Bluffer, judiciously, "he's
nowhere near the proper size of a man, of course. But
he's not ridiculous, like you Shorties. Why, two of
you wouldn't make a half-grown pup. And if people
don't lie, he's strong enough to stand up to a man and
holler for his rights—yes and back them up, too, if he
had to, win or lose."

"That's important?" said John. "To you Dilbians?"

"Why, of course it's important to any man!" said
the Bluffer. "A man might lose. Bound to lose sometime, to someone, of course. But if he stands up for
his rights, then there can't anything worse happen to
him but get killed. I mean, he's got standing in the
community."

"We Shorties stand up for our rights, too," said
John.

"Sure. But—hell!" said the Bluffer. "Besides, what
do you mean, you all stand up for your rights? What
about the Squeaking Squirt?"

"Well . . ." said John, uncomfortably.

He had, for the moment, forgotten Heiner Schlaff,
that blot on the human escutcheon where Dilbia was
concerned. Now, here Schlaff was being thrown in his
face, as he must have been to Joshua on a number of
occasions. For the first time, John felt a twinge of
sympathy with the dapper little ambassador. How do
you go about explaining that one man's reactions are
not typical of a race's?

Attack, thought John.

"Oh, you never knew a man from Dilbia, here, who

lost his head or got scared?" he said.

"I never knew one who yelled just because he was picked up!" snorted the Bluffer.

"Who'd pick one up? Who's big enough to?" said John.

That apparently stopped the Bluffer for a moment. He did not immediately answer.

"You just imagine something big enough to pick you up and tell me if there aren't some men just as big as you who'd lose their head if something like that picked them up?"

"They'd be pretty poor if they did," growled the Bluffer. He muttered to himself for a minute. "Anyway," he said, "that's not the point. The point is, it doesn't matter. It's just plain ridiculous, even if a Shorty like you'd *try* to stand up for his rights. Any idiot could see you wouldn't have a chance against a real man."

"Oh, you think so," said John; wondering what in the galaxy was making him pretend that the Bluffer was not a hundred per cent correct. After a second's thought, he concluded it was probably much the same human-type reaction that had sent Rudi Maltetti diving for the javelin in Brisbane, on the occasion with the Hemnoid ambassador.

The Bluffer snorted with laughter.

"Now," he said, when he had got his humor off his chest, "one of those Fatties, there'd be some point to an argument. But someone like you, why I couldn't take a shove at someone like you. It'd be like swatting a bird."

He brooded for a second.

"Besides," he said. "Some of you Shorties may not be too bad; but a real man doesn't take kindly to critters that got to go around using all kinds of tools for things. Fighting with tools, taking advantage with tools, getting ahead of somebody else by using tools. But particularly fighting with them—that's just plain, downright yellow; the way we see it!"

"Is that so?" said John. "Well, listen to me for a minute—"

"Hold on. Hold on." The Bluffer held up a pacific lump of a hand. "I can't go fighting with my own mail; besides, didn't I say some of you Shorties weren't too bad? Why, you know how Little Bite got his name, and—"

"Who?" said John. And then his hypno training informed him that Little Bite was the Dilbian nickname for Joshua Guy. But the hypno training was silent on how the name had been selected. "Oh, no, I don't."

"You don't?" ejaculated the Bluffer.

"No," said John, suddenly cautious and wondering what he had blundered into.

"Everybody knows that," said the Bluffer.

There was no help for it.

"I don't," said John.

Slowly, the Bluffer turned his head to look back over his shoulder. The eye that met John's was alight with sudden puzzlement and suspicion.

"You're pretty strange, even for a Shorty," said the postman slowly. "What're you trying to pull? Everybody knows how Little Bite got his name. And you're a Shorty yourself and you *don't*?"

He stopped dead in the trail and stood, still staring back at John.

"What're you trying to pull?" he said again.

CHAPTER 7

"Let me down," said John.

"What?" said the Bluffer. "What's that you say?"

"I said," repeated John evenly through his teeth, even though his heart was rising into his throat, "let me down. I've had it."

"Had what?" said the Bluffer; and this time there was more puzzlement than suspicion in his voice.

"I've sat up here," said John, letting his voice climb on a note of anger—not much, but noticeably. "I've sat up here, hung up in this harness and had you insult us Shorties by saying we're all like the Squeaking Squirt. I've had you call me yellow. But I'll be roasted over a slow fire if I have to sit up here and have you imply I'm pulling something just because Little Bite didn't have time to tell me how he got his name. Just let me down and solid ground and by my paternal grandfather—"

"Hey-hey-hey—*hey*!" cried the Bluffer. "I told you I couldn't go around fighting with my mail. What're you getting so hot about?"

"I don't have to take this!" shouted John.

"Well, don't!" shouted the Bluffer. "I didn't mean anything against you, personally. You asked me, didn't you? The smaller they are, the touchier they are! I was just surprised you didn't know how Little

Bite got his name, was all. I was just going to tell you."

"Well, then, why didn't you tell me?" said John in a calmer tone.

"I will—I will!" said the Bluffer, grumpily, taking up the trail again. John relaxed in his saddle and surreptitiously wiped his brow. His hypno training and the Bluffer together had let him know that the Dilbian mail was sacrosanct, but whether that meant from assault by the postman himself, he had not been completely sure, even then. But evidently, even that was true.

"Actually," the Bluffer was saying in a calmer tone, "nearly everybody down at Humrog and through the mountains thinks all right of Little Bite. He's a guest at Humrog, now; and nobody'd dare touch him. But this was back in the first days after he came here—"

A chuckle erupted momentarily into the Bluffer's story.

"—Old Hammertoes, down at Humrog. That old coot's always getting hot about something. Well, he was talking about the good old days, one day. He was drinking some, too. . . ."

John, after the night before at the inn, found himself with a rather graphic mental image of what "drinking a little" might amount to in the case mentioned.

"He was about half loaded, and got himself all riled up over the thought that we had foreigners like Shorties and Fatties all over the place, nowadays. The old world was going to pot, he said; there ought to be a law. He was about half-drunk and he headed up-town."

John's graphic mental image staggered out into the

cobblestone street of Humrog as he remembered it.

"He was all set to put Little Bite—only everybody called him just the Shorty, in those days—back in his shell and kick him clear back into the sky where he came from. Well, he went up and knocked on Little Bite's door. Little Bite opens it; and Hammertoes leans down and shouts in his face:

" 'All right, Shorty! I'm packing you off to your own hole, now!'

"And he made a grab at Little Bite through the door. But Little Bite had this sort of chain on the door so it wouldn't open up all the way; and Hammertoes couldn't get much more than one arm inside. So there he is, half-drunk, hollering 'Come here, you Shorty! You can't get away. I'll get you; and when I get hold of you—' "

John winced. His mental image was becoming so graphic as to be almost painful.

"Then Little Bite, who's picked up something sharp, takes good aim at that big hand of Hammertoes, and cuts Hammertoes a couple times across the knuckles, practically to the bone. Old Hammertoes yells bloody murder and yanks his hand back." The Bluffer began to laugh. "Little Bite slams the door."

The Bluffer was laughing so hard he could not go on. He slowed down and stopped, leaning against the cliff side with one hand while he whooped at the memory. His whole body shook. John held on to his saddle with both hands. It was very disconcerting to be bucked around by the equivalent of a horse that was telling him a funny story at the same time.

"Any—anyway," gasped the Bluffer, getting himself partially back under control, "Old Hammertoes comes back up to the bar, there, dripping blood and sucking on his knuckles.

" 'Why, what happened?' says everybody else at the bar.

" 'Nothing,' says Hammertoes.

" 'Something must've happened. Look at your hand,' says everybody.

" 'I tell you, nothing happened!' yells Hammertoes. 'He wouldn't let me in there where I could grab a hold on him. So I come away. And as for my hand—that's got nothing to do with it. He didn't hurt my hand, hardly at all. All he done was to give it a little bite!' "

The Bluffer went off into another fit of laughter that necessitated stopping and leaning against the cliff. But this time, John found himself laughing too. The story *was* funny—or it seemed funny to John, at least. They laughed together; and when they had both run down, rested a moment in a silence that was almost companionable.

"You know," said the Bluffer, after a moment's silence. "You aren't too bad, for a Shorty."

"You're all right, yourself—for a man," said John.

The Bluffer fell silent again. But he did not move on. After a moment, he sat down on a nearby boulder.

"Climb down," he said, over his shoulder. "I got something to talk to you about; and I can do it better if I'm looking at you while I'm at it."

John frowned, hesitated; but climbed down. He walked around in front of the Dilbian and found that, with the Bluffer seated, and himself standing, they were as close to being eye to eye as they would normally ever expect to be.

"What is it?" asked John.

"You know," said the Bluffer with an effort, "you're not bad for a Shorty as I say and—"

However, having got this far, he was stuck. It was rather hard for a human like John to read embarrassment on a Dilbian face; but if such a thing was possible, John thought he spotted that emotion on the Hill Bluffer now. He avoided the postman's eyes and simply waited. Looking off past the big head, he saw, far beyond the sharp mountain peaks, a few white puffs of clouds, looking peaceful and innocent.

"What I mean is," said the Bluffer finally, after an apparent inner struggle. "The Streamside Terror's had his drinking mug spilt."

For a moment, John did not understand. And then he did, his hypno training coming once more to the rescue. To have one's drinking mug spilt, in Dilbian terms, was to endure a deadly affront to personal honor. In short, someone had given the Streamside Terror reason for starting a blood feud. John had a sinking feeling as to whom it might be.

"By me?" said John. "But he's never seen me."

"No. By Little Bite," said the Bluffer. "But you're sort of hauled into it. It's real peculiar."

"I'll bet," said John, thinking about the small ambassador back at Humrog.

"You see," said the Bluffer, "Little Bite's a guest at Humrog nowadays."

"I know. You told me," said John.

"Let me finish. Now, since he's a guest, his fights are Humrog's fights. But Little Bite shamed the Terror, when he told old Shaking Knees the Terror shouldn't be let have Boy Is She Built. Because that meant the Terror was being called not worthy. Well, now what's the Terror going to do? He can't get mad at Shaking Knees for not letting him have Boy Is She Built. A man's got a right to look out for his daughter. He could get mad at Little Bite; but nobody in his right mind—even somebody like Streamside—is going to start a blood feud with a town of five thousand.

"I mean, Clan Hollows could back him up, and that's more of a match; but Clan Hollows would be crazy if they did—when most of the stuff they sell gets sold in and to Humrog. No, what'd happen is that the grandfathers of Clan Hollows'd declare it a personal matter and Streamside'd have a choice of hiding out in Clan Hollows territory for the rest of his life, or being hung up by the heels before the year was out."

"I see," said John. And he did. He was thinking deeply. Up until this point he had simply refused to accept the notion that Joshua could be deliberately at fault in sending him out on this mission. Mistakenly so, that was imaginable. But to plan to draft a man and send him out to cover up what had evidently been a diplomatic error on the little man's part—it was staggering. Men of sufficient stature to be appointed ambassadors, particularly to posts like this, did just not descend to such unethical tactics to hide their dirty linen. The job Joshua had given John to do was absolutely illegal; and John was under absolutely no compulsion to go through with it.

He opened his mouth to say so, to tell the Bluffer that they should return immediately to Humrog—and closed it again, slowly, without having uttered a word. He had suddenly remembered how cleverly Joshua had him trapped. The Bluffer would certainly not just turn around on John's say-so and head back for the town. He had contracted to deliver a piece of mail to the Streamside Terror; and his Dilbian honor was at stake.

The Hill Bluffer had been waiting the several seconds it took John to think this out. Now, he opened his large mouth again, and put a further aspect of the matter out for John's consideration.

"You know," said the Bluffer. "You can't get Greasy Face back from the Terror without fighting him?"

The words went in John's ears and knocked the problem of Joshua clear back out of sight.

"*Fighting* him??" he echoed.

"Yep," said the Bluffer. "Man-to-man. No weapons. No holds barred."

John blinked. He looked past the postman's head at the puffs of white clouds. They had not moved. They were still there. So were the mountains. It must be something wrong with his ears.

"Fighting him?" said John again, feeling like a man in a fast elevator which has just begun to descend.

"A man's got his pride," said the Bluffer. "If you take Greasy Face back, his mug's spilt all over again." He leaned a little toward John. "That is, unless you whip him in a fair fight. Then there's no blood feud to it. You're just a better man than he is, that's all. But that's why I haven't been able to figure this. You aren't bad for a Shorty. You pulled a good trick with that beer on those drunks last night. You got guts."

He looked searchingly at John.

"But I mean—Hell, you can't fight the Terror. Anybody'd know that. I mean—*Hell*!" said the Bluffer, explosively finding his vocabulary insufficient to describe his overcharged feelings.

John was wishing he could express to the postman

how much he agreed with him.

"So what," inquired the Bluffer, "are you going to do when I deliver you to Streamside?"

John thought about it. He took a deep breath and blew it out again.

"I don't know," he said, at last.

"Well, not my problem," said the Bluffer, getting to his feet. "Go on around and climb on by the rock, there. Oh, by the way," he added as John followed this instruction. "Know who it was pitched you over the cliff last night?"

"Who?" asked John. He had explained the evening adventures and his waking up to the Hill Bluffer over the morning beer; but the Bluffer had made no comment, then.

"The Cobbly Queen. You on, back there?"

"Yes. Who?" said John, remembering how the woodsman had winked at them while mentioning the same mythical character yesterday.

"Boy" said the Bluffer, a little grimly, "Is She Built. The same little wagtail that sends postmen messages to make a five mile sidetrip to pick up special mail, while she's back at the inn monkeying with the mail he was carrying to start off with. I'd sure like," said the Bluffer, "to figure out how she could leave with enough head start to be there ahead of us, and still know that was where we were going."

So, thought John, pricking up his ears at this information, did he.

"Well, let's go."

And the Hill Bluffer swung off again once more down the trail. Swinging and bouncing in the saddle on the Dilbian's broad back, John mulled over this new information that had just been supplied him. It occurred to him that it might be a wise idea, on all accounts to phone Joshua Guy back at Humrog, and let the ambassador know John had just uncovered the whole of his seamy little scheme.

There was no doubt now that Joshua Guy, inadvertently or not, had got himself into a bad diplomatic situation with the Streamside Terror with his advice to the father of Boy Is She Built. It had been none of the human's business to begin with whom Boy Is She Built got paired off with. In fact, it was just this sort of monkeying in private alien affairs that had gotten humanity in hot water before. A human representative who goofed like that stood in a fair way of being chopped, himself, back home once the news got out, and provided it could be proved against him. Blunders like that had cost human lives before and might well again.

It came home to John, suddenly, with a repetition of the elevator feeling he had experienced a little before, that one of the lives it might cost in this instance might well be his own.

For if John met the Terror and got mashed, it might solve several things at once for Joshua Guy.

In the first place, it would probably save Greasy Face, since the Terror would have no further reason for holding on to her after his shame had been washed out in John's blood; and Shaking Knees had given the successful warrior Boy Is She Built, after all, as he would be practically obligated to do so under Dilbian mores. That would get Joshua off the hot spot where the life of the female human sociologist was concerned. Also, it would dispose of the only one, John again, who knew what Joshua had been up to and could bring human charges against him. Moreover, it

would allow him to sidetrack any blame in the affair
by pinning it on John's mismanagement of matters
after John had left Humrog.

And the Hill Bluffer was carrying John inexorably
to the destination Joshua had planned for him. There
was no hope of turning the Dilbian postman.

There was, however, one thing John could do. He
could call Joshua on the wrist phone and make it
clear that unless Joshua somehow pulled him and
Greasy Face out of this, John would spread word
among the Dilbians about what was going on. After
that, it would be merely a matter of time before the
news leaked past Joshua and back to authorities on
Earth. A good bluff might get Joshua out here to
mend things on the double. After all, if he could stop
things now, there would be no capital crime such as
would be involved if the Terror killed John or Greasy
Face. Joshua would be a fool not to stop things.

Cooled by a sudden rush of relief, John lifted his
wrist to his lips. It was then that he noticed something.

The long gouge in his left forearm ran right down
under where the strap to his wrist phone had gone
around his wrist. And, wherever the wrist phone was
now, John, at least, no longer had it.

CHAPTER 8

THERE are times when the imagination simply gives up. It happened that way with John about this time. It was, he knew, a temporary thing—or he hoped it was—which possibly a good night's sleep or a bit of unexpected luck, or some such thing, could snap him out of. But for the moment, the intellectual, hardworking part of his brain had hung up a notice "Out —Back later" and gone off for a nap.

He simply could not think constructively. Whenever he tried to figure out a way out of his present situation, he came back around to the fact that the Hill Bluffer, whether John liked it or not, was taking him—and nothing could stop the process—directly to the Streamside Terror, who—and nothing could stop that, either—would pick John up and effectively kill him. It was written. Kismet. Give up.

John did. In the end, he slumped in the saddle and dozed.

A sudden stopping on the part of the Hill Bluffer woke John with a start. He sat up and looked around him.

At first he saw nothing but a gorge with vertical sides of light, salmon-colored granite and a thread of a river away down at its base. Then he realized that he was looking over the edge of a ledge that the Bluffer was standing on and he readjusted the angle of his view.

Having done this, he saw that the ledge was actually almost as large as the widening of the road had been at Brittle Rock Inn, only they were standing at the very edge of it. At this edge was one end of a suspension bridge that swooped breathtakingly across the open space of the gorge to a landing on a smaller ledge on the far side. Its further end was anchored high on the face of the rock wall behind the further ledge, where the trail took up again.

At this end there was a small log hut, outside which the Hill Bluffer was now in conversation with a hefty-looking, middle-aged Dilbian.

"Saw him turn off at the fork myself!" this Dilbian was bellowing. "You questioning the word of a public official? Want me to swear on my winch-cable? Eh?" He laid a heavy, pawlike hand on the great drum on which the cables of the bridge were wound, crank-driven through a series of carved wooden gears by a polished wooden handle.

"I was just asking!" roared the Bluffer. "A man can ask, can't he?"

"If he asks politely, all right," said the evident bridgekeeper, stubbornly. "I said I seen him turn off at the fork on this side and go over the bridge there." He pointed along this side of the gorge and John saw where, on this side the trail did split, one way following along the near cliff face, and the other crossing the bridge disappearing through a cleft in the rock. "He headed toward the high country and Ice Dog Glacier."

"All right. All right, I believe you!" said the Bluffer. He turned toward the bridge.

"Hey," said the bridgekeeper. "Your toll."

"Toll!"

The Bluffer spun about in outrage.

"Me? A government postman? Toll?"

"Well," grumbled the other, "after doubting my word like that, I'd think you'd want—"

"Toll!" snorted the Bluffer, in contempt, and turning about, marched off over the bridge without waiting for the bridgekeeper to finish.

"Are we going someplace different?" asked John, as they left the far end of the bridge, and headed into the cleft in the rock.

"Streamside's headed for glacier country," muttered the Bluffer. "Or maybe he plans to double over the mountains the other way at Halfway House, and end up in the Free Forest. Anyway we got to shake a leg to catch him, if that's it. *Toll!*"

He snorted again and put on speed.

Their new road took them steeply up and away from the territory of rivers and deep gorges. After half an hour's climb they began to emerge into an area of wide, stony slopes across which a high-altitude wind blew with the sort of coolness that did not permit sleeping in the saddle.

It was past noon when they came around a bend in the slope three hours later and approached another inn. This one, situated to take advantage of what little natural shelter there was in this exposed area, was built almost exclusively of stone and earth. They stopped for a midday break, and John got down to stretch his legs gratefully. His brain was still refusing to make itself useful by coming up with any plan to frustrate the ambassador; but the cool, keen winds had blown John into physical wakefulness, so much

so that he realized he was tired of the saddle. If it had
not been clearly an impractical notion, John would
have liked to forego riding and walk for a while.

But there was no hope of that. If John should try to
make it on foot, the Bluffer would be over the horizon
and out of sight inside of half an hour. That is, unless
he held his pace down to that of his human companion. And, numb-minded as he was at the moment,
John had to smile at the thought of the explosive and
impatient Bluffer's reaction, if he was asked to do
that.

So, John made the best of it by taking a stroll
around the stone inn of Halfway House to take the
kinks out of his leg muscles. When he approached the
front door of it again, he found the Bluffer on the
point of explosion. The cause of this was not John, or
anything he had done, but the other visitors at the
Halfway House.

They were laughing at the Bluffer.

There were half a dozen of them just outside the
door of the House, headed by a relatively short and
chunky Dilbian carrying a sort of alpenstock.

"Hor! Hor!" the short Dilbian was bellowing.

"You want to make something out of it?" the Bluffer was roaring.

"What is it?" asked John. Nobody even heard him,
of course.

"Fixed you right!" chortled the short Dilbian.

"Fixed me. . . .! I'll show who fixed me!" The Bluffer shook both fists high over his head. It was an
awesome sight. "Swore to me as a public official, he
did. Said he'd seen the Terror take the fork this way
with his own two eyes!"

"He did! Sure he did!" put in somebody else. "Tell
him, Snowshoe!"

"Why," said the chunky Dilbian, "he saw the Terror take the right fork, all right. But after that he closed his eyes for a bit there, just like she'd arranged."

"She?" bellowed the Bluffer. "Boy Is She Built?"

"Why, who else, postman? The Terror was waiting for her to catch up with him there.

" 'That long-legged postman's right behind me,' she says.

" 'Don't, now,' she says. 'You can't fight the government mail,' she says. 'I got a better idea.' And she fixed it up with old Winchrope to close his eyes while they come back out of one fork and took the other to the Hollows with that female Shorty they had along." The chunky Dilbian named Snowshoes stopped to laugh again. "Passing by myself at the time. Saw the whole thing. Laugh! Thought I'd split a gut!"

The Bluffer bellowed to the mountain sky. His eyes fell on John and he snatched John up like the package John was officially supposed to be.

The next thing they knew, they were fifteen yards back along the trail they had just come, and gaining speed.

"Hey!" said John. "At least let me get in the saddle."

"What? Oh!" snarled the Bluffer. He checked and waited a few impatient seconds, while John crawled over his shoulder into the saddle. Then he took off again.

Two hours later they were back at the wrong end of the bridge. The word wrong was, thought John, used advisedly. For the bridge was now out of their reach.

What had been done was simple enough. Their end of the bridge had its cables fastened to the sheer cliff face some twenty feet back and another twenty feet above their heads. What had been done was to tighten these cables by means of the winch to which they were attached at their other end. The sag of the span had straightened out, lifting the bridge up and out of their reach.

The Hill Bluffer bellowed across the gap. His first forty words were a description of Winchrope's person and morals, his last four an order to put the bridge back down where he and John could reach it, and cross.

There was no answer at the far end. The windlass to which the cables were attached showed no inclination to comply with the order by itself and no one emerged from the bridgekeeper's hut.

"What's happened?" asked John.

"He's in there!" raged the Bluffer. "That bridge isn't supposed to be cranked up until night—and then only to keep people from sneaking across and not paying their toll. He's in there, all right. He just won't come out and let it down, because he knows what I'll do to him the minute I get over there." He thundered across the gorge again. "Get out here and let down this unmentionable, indescribable bridge, so I can get over it at you and tear your head off!"

The bridgekeeper still showed no eagerness to take the Bluffer up on this invitation. Small wonder, thought John privately, standing prudently back out of arms reach of the wrought-up postman.

The Bluffer stopped shouting and looked up at the bridge overhead. He made a half-hearted motion as if to try reaching for it; but it was obviously many feet beyond even the stretch of his long arms. He dropped them, defeatedly.

"All right!" he roared once more, shaking his fist across the gorge. "I'll climb up along the gorge. I'll go along the cliff. I don't need a trail. I'll get to the Hollows before Streamside does! And then I'm coming back for you!"

John stirred suddenly, pricked for the first time out of his mental lethargy.

"Go up the gorge?" he said.

"You heard me!" growled the Bluffer. "Who needs a trail? It's the shortest route. We'll get there in half the time."

John glanced over the Bluffer's shoulder at the sheer walls of the gorge on the edge of which they were standing. There were footholds along it, all right, but even for someone of the Bluffer's skill. And then there was that business of catching up with Streamside faster than expected. John came fully awake.

"Lift me up," he said to postman. "If I can reach, and climb across and let the winch out—"

The Bluffer's eyes lit up.

"Sure," he said, enthusiastically. He picked up John and they tried it. John, upheld by the ankles and holding his body stiff, stretched upward toward the bare cable near the end of the bridge's flooring slats, but was rewarded only by a throat-squeezing view of the Knobby River, nine hundred feet below.

"Put me down," he said at last. The Hill Bluffer put him down.

John, not in the most cheerful mood in the universe after his scenic view of the gorge, went over and examined the cliff face leading up to the anchor points of the bridge cables. He possessed a fair amount of rock climbing experience and the granite face before

him was not too bad, although no one of the bulk and
necessary clumsiness of a Dilbian could have made it.
It was not that, so much, that was giving him cold
shivers, as the fact that once he had reached an anchor point, he would have to work out along the bare
cable some twenty-odd feet before he came to the
bridge proper.

Oh, well, he thought.

"Hey! Where're you going?" shouted the Bluffer.

John did not answer. He needed his breath and
anyway his destination was obvious. After a little
time, he reached the near anchor point, and got his
arms over the rough, three-inch cable. He rested for a
moment and surveyed the situation. The Bluffer was
just below him, staring up and looking foreshortened
by the angle of John's vision. So was the ledge. John
did not look down into the gorge.

After a while, he got his breath back and he
climbed up with both arms and legs wrapped around
the cable, himself on top, and began to inch his way
toward the bridge end, floating in an absurdly large
amount of space at a remarkable distance from him.
It occurred to him, after he had covered about six or
eight feet in this fashion, that a real hero in this situation would undoubtedly have got to his feet and
tightrope-walked the really rather broad cable to the
end of the bridge proper. This, in addition to impress-
ing the watching Hill Bluffer, would have shortened
the time of personal suspense considerably.

John concluded that evidently he was just not the
stuff out of which real heroes are made, and continued to inch along.

Eventually, he reached the bridge, crawled out on it
and lay panting for a while, then got up and crossed

to the far side of the gorge. The far ledge of the gorge was still the home of somebody dodging a process server. John walked over to the winch, and utilizing a handy rock, managed to knock loose the lock-rachet.

The winch roared loose, the cables boomed like gigantic bowstrings; and the far end of the bridge slammed down, raising a temporary cloud of dust through which the Hill Bluffer was shortly to be seen advancing with a look of grim purpose. He stalked passed John and entered the bridgekeeper's abode. Without knocking.

There was a moment of silence; and then sound erupted like a bomb exploding inside the hut.

John looked hastily around for something to climb up on or inside of, where he would be out of harm's way. He had never seen a pair of Dilbians fight; but it was remarkable how accurately his ears interpreted what was going on inside the hut right now.

After a little while, abruptly, there was peace. The Hill Bluffer emerged, dabbing with one big hand at a torn ear, but otherwise looking not unsatisfied.

"What happened?" asked John.

The Bluffer went over and washed off his ear in a large stone trough that ran along side the shack.

"Said it was *his* bridge. Hah!" replied the Bluffer. "Nobody stops the mail. I fixed him." He paused, water dripping from one side of his big head and looked over at John. "You did all right, too, Half-Pint."

"Me?" said John.

"Climbing up and out across that cable to the bridge. Never thought I'd see a Shorty, even a good one, doing something like that. Actually took a little guts, I'd say. All right. Climb up and let's get going."

John complied.

"You didn't kill him?" he asked as they headed off up their original fork of the trail toward the Hollows.

"Who? Old Winchrope? Just knocked a little sense into him. Hell, there's got to be somebody around here keep the bridge up and in repair. Hang on. It's all downhill from here, and we're late. But it'll be twilight in two hours and I think we can just make Sour Ford by then."

And the Hill Bluffer, swinging once again into his six-foot, ground-devouring stride, was once more hot on the trail of the Terror.

CHAPTER 9

THEY made good time.

As the Bluffer had said, from there on it was all downhill. They descended almost immediately into the treed sections of the mountains, the forest part. The trees among which they now traveled were lofty and thick-topped. All underbrush between them had been killed off by the lack of sunlight and they traveled, through what seemed to be an endlessly, sloping, pillared land, dimly lit by no particular source of illumination.

Sound was less where they were, too. There were no insects to feed on the nonexistent small vegetation; and no birds to live off the insects. Occasionally, from high overhead, eighty to a hundred and twenty feet up in the loftily remote crowns of the trees, there would float down a distant chitter or chirp of some unseen animal or winged creature. Otherwise, there was only the trail, an occasional boulder, looking lost here in the wooded dimness, and the unending carpet of dead leaf forms from the trees.

The Bluffer said nothing; and the steady rocking of his body as he swung along over the trail, now soft with earth, swayed John into a dreaminess in which nothing about him seemed real. Not the present scene, and not the whole business in which he had become engaged, seemed to have anything to do with reality. What was he doing here, strapped up on the back of an alien individual as large as a horse and headed for a duel to the death with another horse-sized individual of the same race? Such things did not happen to ordinary people.

But, come to think of it, were there any ordinary people? When you got right down to it, thought John sleepily, nobody was ordinary.

John dozed. An indeterminate, grey time went past; and then he was awakened by the jerk of the Hill Bluffer stopping. He straightened up, blinking, and looked about him.

He saw that it was already dusk. In the fading light, they stood in a large grassy clearing semi-encircled by the forest trees. Directly before him was a long, low log building at least double the size of anything he had seen yet, outside of Humrog. At some short distance behind it, a broad, smooth-surfaced river gurgled, swiftly flowing around a chin of stones that led off across it to be lost in the twilight and the tree shadow on the far side of the stream.

"Light down, Half-Pint," said the Bluffer.

Stiffly, John climbed down from the harness. His scrapes and bruises of the night before, had found time to set during his long hours in the saddle. The soft turf felt odd under his bootsoles and his calves were wooden with a mild cramp. He stamped about, restoring his circulation; and then followed the Hill Bluffer's great back as, for an instant, it blocked out the yellow light of an open doorway, in passing into the building's interior.

Inside he found himself in a common room both much larger and much cleaner than he had been in before. The customers here at Sour Ford Inn also seemed to be quieter and less drunk than those he had encountered in other Dilbian inns, Brittle Rock for example. Gazing around for some explanation of the reason behind this difference, John caught sight of a raised dais at the far end of the room, where in a huge chair was seated a truly enormous Dilbian, grizzled with age and heavy with fat.

Staring at this Dilbian as he walked behind the Bluffer, John ran into a table, recovered himself, and was admonished by the Hill Bluffer.

"Don't go starting any trouble now, Half-Pint."

"Me?" said John, so overwhelmed at the suggestion that someone his size could start trouble with lumbering Dilbians—even if he was crazy enough to want to—that he found himself at a loss for words to protest properly that he had no such intention.

"That's right," said the Bluffer, some moments later, after they had been seated and ordered beer and food (beer only, still, for John). "This here's treaty ground, belonging to a clanless man. Nobody starts trouble here."

"Treaty ground?"

"Yep," said the Hill Bluffer. "One Man, he—" the food, arriving just then, put a cork in the postman's flow of words. He devoted himself to bread, cheese and beer, merely grunting when John tried to continue the conversation.

John sat back, and sipped on his beer. He was cautious with it, this evening. He tried to catch a glimpse of the big Dilbian at the room's end, through the shifting bodies passing in and about the tables in the room, but the way was never clear long enough for him to get a good look.

Suddenly, however, John dropped his mug with a bang on the table and sat bolt upright.

"Hey!" he said, punching the Bluffer.

The Bluffer took another large bite of meat.

"*Hey!*" said John, punching harder.

The Bluffer growled something unintelligible with his mouth full.

"Look up!" said John. "Look over there! Quick!"

The Hill Bluffer looked up, in the direction John was pointing. He did not seem disturbed to see a Hemnoid accompanied by a relatively short, plump Dilbian female, threading their way between the tables toward the enormous patriarch in the chair on the dais.

The Bluffer swallowed.

"Sure," he said, casually. "That's that Fatty, Tark-*ay*. The one I was telling you about claims to be quite a scrapper back on his home world?" The Bluffer discovered he needed to dispose of one more swallow, and did so. He pointed with a large finger, while picking up a large chunk of bread with his other hand. "That's Boy Is She Built with him."

"Boy Is She Built?" John stared.

"That's what they all say," muttered the Bluffer through a mouthful of bread. "Like 'em a little skinnier, myself."

"I mean—" said John. "What's she doing here? Let's go get her and make her tell us about Greasy Face, and if Greasy Face is all right—"

"Now, there you go," said the Bluffer.

"Go?" John turned to blink at him.

"Starting trouble."

"Starting trouble?"

"Didn't," said the Bluffer, "I just finish telling you

this here's treaty ground? Man's got to be polite on treaty ground. Everybody, even Shorties got to respect the rules."

John fell silent. The Bluffer went back to his eating. John watched the Hemnoid, Tark-*ay,* and Boy Is She Built who proceeded up to the dais, sat down; and evidently fell into a friendly conversation with the oversize patriarch seated there.

John wished he could hear what they were saying.

He looked over at the Bluffer, eating away; and began to try to evolve some kind of scheme which would inveigle the Bluffer into taking him over to meet the giant Dilbian, in turn. And as soon as the Bluffer was finished, John took a cautious sip of beer and went to work.

"Who did you say is that man down in the chair at the end?" he asked.

"Why, don't you know? No, I guess you don't," said the Bluffer. "Why, that's One Man, Half-Pint. This here's all his, at Sour Ford."

"Quite a man," said John.

"You can say that," replied the Bluffer judiciously, draining the last drops from his beer mug.

"I'd like a meet a man like that," said John. "Now, back home—"

"That's good," said the Bluffer, standing up. "Because the waitress passed word I was to bring you over, soon as we were through eating. Come on, Half-Pint."

He headed off between the tables. John shook his head ruefully and followed. The next time, he thought, I'll ask first and scheme afterwards.

When they got close to the individual in the chair, John discovered that sometime during their passage

across the room, the Hemnoid and Boy Is She Built
had disappeared. He did not have much opportunity
to wonder about this, however; because his attention
was immediately completely taken up by the Dilbian
he was about to meet. One Man was that sort of a
being.

It was definitely disconcerting, after John had spent
a couple of days adjusting to the idea of Dilbian size,
to have that adjustment knocked for a fresh row of
pins. He was rather like a man who having gotten
used to measuring with a yardstick instead of a foot-
rule, suddenly finds the yardstick replaced by a
fathom line. And he, himself as a fraction of that
measurement getting smaller and smaller.

John had accustomed himself to standing about
armpit high on the ordinary male Dilbian. Now, here
along came a specimen on which John could hardly
hope to stand more than midrib height. John's reaction was rather like Gulliver's with the Brobding-
nagians. He felt like standing on tiptoe and shouting
to make himself heard.

One Man overflowed the massive chair in which he
sat; and the greying hair on the top of his head almost
brushed against a polished, six-foot staff of hardwood
laid crosswise on pegs driven into the wall six feet
above the floor, behind him. His massive forearms
and great pawlike hands were laid out on the small
table in front of him, like swollen clubs of bone and
muscle. Attendant Dilbians stood respectfully about
him. He looked like some overstuffed, barbaric
potentate. Yet his large, grey eyes, meeting John's
suddenly and sharply as John and the Bluffer came to
stand before him, were alight with an unusual quality
of penetrating intelligence.

It was the look John had noticed back home on earth, in the eyes of human politicians of statesman level.

"This here's the Half-Pint Posted, One Man," said the Hill Bluffer, as the Dilbians around passed forth a bench for him and John to sit on. The Bluffer sat down. John climbed up to sit beside him.

"Welcome, Half-Pint," rumbled One Man. His voice was so deep with its chest tones that it sounded like a great drum sounding somewhere off in the forest. "This is the moment we've all been waiting for."

CHAPTER 10

"You've been waiting for me?" John stared at the big Dilbian.

"To be sure," said One Man. "No Shorty has ever been a guest under this roof before." He bent his head with solemn dignity in John's direction. It was all very pompous and empty-sounding; but John got the sudden clear conviction that One Man's first words had been plainly intended to give a double meaning. What was it? A warning? John flicked his eyes about as much as he could without actually turning his head away to look; but he saw nothing but unusually well-mannered Dilbian faces. Tark-*ay* and Boy Is She Built were still not in evidence.

"It's a pleasure to be here," John was saying, meanwhile, automatically.

"You're my guest under this roof," said One Man. "For now and at any time in the future, if you come back."

Again, there was that impression of a double meaning. John was completely baffled as to what there was in what One Man said, or possibly in the way he said it, that was giving him the hint of some undercover message. Also, why would the giant Dilbian be doing such a thing? He undoubtedly did not know John from Adam, or any other Shorty.

"Has the Bluffer told you about me?" One Man was asking.

"Well, not much—"

"It's probably just as well." The enormous head nodded mildly. "The past is the past; and I'm an old man dreaming in my chair, here. . . ."

John just bet he was. From what he had seen of Dilbians, they did not accord the sort of respect he was witnessing to any ancient hulk, no matter how venerable.

"They call him One Man, Half-Pint," put in the Bluffer, "because he once held blood feud all alone— being an orphan—with a whole clan. And won!"

"Ah, yes. The old days," rumbled One Man, with a faraway look in his eyes.

"One time," said the Bluffer, "five of them caught him on a trail where there wasn't any chance to get away. He killed them all."

"Luck was with me, of course," said One Man modestly. "Well, well, I don't want to bring up past exploits. It'll be more polite to talk about my guest. Tell me, Half-Pint," the grey eyes suddenly came penetrating, zeroing in on John, "what are you Shorties doing here, anyway?"

John blinked.

"Well," he said, "I'm here looking for—er— Greasy Face, myself."

"Of course." One Man nodded benignly. "But what brought her, and the others?" His eyes went dreamily away from John out over the room. "There must be some plan, you'd think." He looked quizzically back at John. "Nobody asked you all to come here, you know."

"Well, no," said John. He felt definitely at a loss.

The Diplomatic Service had people like Joshua Guy
trained to explain the reasons for human expansion
into space. He summoned up what he could remember of his high school civics; and tried to present
this to One Man in Dilbian terms. One Man nodded
agreeably; but John had a hunch he was not making
many points. What, for example, could population pressure mean to a Dilbian to whom a community of five thousand was a big city? And what could
"the automatic spread of civilization" convey,
other than the sound of some large and complicated words?

"That's very interesting now, Half-Pint," said One
Man, when John had finally run down." "But you
know what kind of puzzles me about you Shorties,"
he leaned forward confidentially, "is why you figure
people ought to like you."

"Why, we don't—" began John, and then suddenly
realized that humans did. It was one of the outstanding—if not the most outstanding—human character-
istics. "I guess we do. All right, what's wrong with
that? We're prepared to like other people."

One Man nodded sagely.

"I hadn't thought of that, Half-Pint," he said sol-
emnly. "Of course, that explains it." He looked
around at the other Dilbians. "Naturally, they expect
people to like them, if they like people. Maybe we
should have realized that."

The other Dilbians looked back at him in apparent
puzzlement. But evidently they were used to being
puzzled by this oversize patriarch because nobody ob-
jected. John, on his part, frowned; not sure whether
he was being made fun of or not.

"I just can't make up my mind about you Shorties," said One Man, with a sigh. It was like a moun-

tain sighing. "Well, well, I'm not being much of a host, making my guest here dig around for the reasons behind things; when I ought to be thinking only of entertaining him. Let's see now, what would be instructive and pleasant. . . ." He lifted a big finger suddenly. "I've got it. It's been a long time since I broke my stick for anyone. Will one of you, there, hand it down to me?"

A young Dilbian at one side got up, lifted down the staff from the pegs above One Man's head; and gave it to One Man, who took the six-foot, three-inch-thick young post in both hands. He held it crosswise before him with his hands about three feet apart and his wrists flat on the table before him.

"A little trick of mine," he said confidentially to John. "You might get a kick out of it." He closed his fists firmly about the pole. Then, without moving his arms in any way or lifting his wrists from the table, he twisted both fists to the outside.

The thick hardwood curved up in the center like a strung bow—and snapped.

One Man leaned forward and handed the pieces to John. They were heavy and awkward enough so that John preferred to tuck them under one arm.

"Souvenir for you," said One Man, quietly.

John nodded his thanks, a little numbly. What he had just witnessed was impossible. Even for a Dilbian. Even for a Dilbian like One Man. The lack of leverage forced by the requirement of keeping wrists flat with the table, made it impossible.

"No man except me ever was able to do that," said One Man, closing his eyes dreamily. "Good luck with the Terror, Half-Pint."

John still sat where he was, staring at the broken ends of the wood pieces under his arm, until the Bluf-

fer tapped him on the shoulder and led him off
through the room, through another hide curtain and
into a long room furnished with two rows of springy
branches from the conifer-type trees of the forest outside the inn. The mounds made effective natural
springs and mattresses for sleepers. A number of male
Dilbians were already slumbering along the room.
The Bluffer led John to a mound of branches in the
far corner.

"You can turn in here, Half-Pint," he said.
"Nobody'll bother you here." He pointed toward the
entrance. "I'll be out there, if you want to find me."

The mound of branches suddenly looked very good
to John. He was bone-weary. He laid the pieces of
broken staff that One Man had given him, down
beside the mound and sat down on it to take off his
shoes.

Five minutes later, he was asleep.

At some indeterminate time after that, he awoke
suddenly and with all senses alert. For a long moment
he merely lay tense and waiting, ears straining, as if
for the warning of an instant attack.

But no attack came. After a moment, he sat up
cautiously and looked around him.

In the light of the single thick candle burning by the
entrance he saw that the dormitory was now full of
sleepers. The Dilbians all slumbered with a silence
that was amazing, considering their size and their
boisterousness during waking hours. Beside John the
Hill Bluffer was now asleep on a neighboring mound,
lying on his side with one great hairy arm outflung,
palm up. But it was hardly possible to tell that the
postman was breathing.

John sat looking around the dormitory, trying to imagine what had wakened him. But there was nothing to see. He was isolated and undisturbed. Even his shoes, and One Man's broken staff lay just where John had laid them, beside the mound of branches.

Yet, John's tenseness continued.

The more he thought of it now, the more convinced he was that One Man had been trying to convey some message or other to him under the mask of casual conversation. The giant Dilbian was without a doubt vastly more intelligent than those around him. Also he seemed to occupy a unique position.

John swore softly to himself.

He had just remembered something that had been niggling at the back of his mind ever since he had walked into the Sour Ford Inn and seen the seated shape of its proprietor. One of the reasons One Man had attracted John's attention was that he had looked familiar. And he had looked familiar because John had seen him before—or at least his image.

One Man had been the oversize Dilbian in the cube of the three-dimensional on Joshua Guy's desk in Humrog.

That did it.

Now what was he supposed to think, wondered John bleakly. One Man—friend or foe? If the giant Dilbian was a close friend of Joshua's—and if he was not a close friend of Joshua's, what was the three-dimensional of him doing on Joshua's desk?

John shoved a hand distractedly through his ruffled mass of red hair. As a boy he had eagerly read not only *The Three Musketeers,* and *Twenty Years After,* but everything dealing with Dumas' famous musketeers. Then he had envied D'Artagnan and his three sworded friends for dashing about risking their lives by engaging in high intrigue. Now, fifteen years later and spang in the middle of a similar adventure, he realized they all must have been nuts, to say the least. Like the hired hand in the joke who could plow four hundred acres with ease but had a hard time sorting potatoes, it wasn't the risks in adventure that got you down. It was the decisions.

And this business about the broken staff. Why give the pieces to John? A souvenior, One Man had said; and possibly this was true from the Dilbian point of view, but it was hardly the kind of present for a Shorty headed for battle *a l'outrance* with a Terror.

John reached down and hefted up the two pieces for another look. It was still impossible, he thought once more, as he examined the broken ends. Physical strength alone just wasn't enough.

He checked suddenly and bent to examine the break more closely. There seemed to be a faint stain covering most of the interior area of each broken end. It radiated out around a faint line that went from the edge into the center. In the dim light he bent close over the line, but could make nothing out. He rubbed the tip of his finger over it; it was a faint groove. He put the two ends back together and the grooves matched.

It occurred to John that it would not be too impossible to drill a tiny hole into the center of even a fairly large staff. Then if some corrosive liquid was poured down this hole at intervals over a period of time, it could well result in a definite weakness in the wood at that point. In fact, with experimentation, it might be possible to control the degree of weakness, so that only someone with unusual strength to begin with. . . .

Hmm, thought John. He began to consider One Man in a new light.

Now, if I had brains as well as brawn, thought John, in a physically oriented society—and if I was alone in the world, so that these two things were all that I had to go on, what would I do?

Play down the brains and play up the brawn, of course, he answered himself. I might even build myself into a living legend with supernormal attributes, if I was clever; and so give myself protection in my old age when my strength would begin to dwindle.

Query: If I was this sort of individual, would I enter into any associations or alliances with any other individuals or groups?

Answer: No, I wouldn't dare. Too close an association with anyone else would destroy the illusion of supernormality which was my best protection.

Ergo, thought John, One Man could not be on Joshua's side. Or on the Terror's. In which case, it was just barely possible to persuade him to be on John's.

John put on his shoes and got quietly to his feet. It would not be a bad idea, he thought, to hunt up One Man right now and see if they could not have a further, and more private, chat about things.

He went softly down the long length of the dormitory and out through the hide curtain into the common room.

There were few Dilbians left at the tables; and One Man's chair was empty. He had not taken one of the branch-mounds in the dormitory; so either he had separate quarters elsewhere, or perhaps he did not sleep here at the inn. John stood a moment, irresolutely. The few Dilbians in the room were ignoring him, by reason of that particular blindness to someone his size that he had encountered before. They simply were not expecting to see anyone built that close to the ground. In a literal sense, they were all looking over his head.

It occurred to John that One Man might still be around, but have stepped outside, or retired to one of the smaller houses or whatever they were behind the inn. Quietly—after his experience at Brittle Rock Inn he had no wish to call attention to himself—he crossed the room, pushed the heavy hide curtain aside and slipped out.

Outside, he paused to accustom his eyes to the night, moving a little way off from the inn to get away from the door and window light. Slowly, the starlit scene took shape around him, solidifying out of obscurity. The wide face of the river ran silver-dark in the faint light, and the distant woods loomed like the tidal wave of some black sea. The clearing where the Inn and the outbuildings behind it stood, lay pooled in silence.

He turned and found his way cautiously around the main building to its back. Unlike the Brittle Rock establishment, the backyard area here, sloping gradually to the river, was clear of rubbish; and the outbuildings themselves were neatly in good repair. Between them, when the way was close, the shadows were deeper and John had almost to feel his way.

It occurred to him then—and he wondered why he had not thought of it before—that a good share of these were probably private living quarters, not only for One Man, but for the rest of his staff, as well as any female visitors. Females seemed to have little to do with Dilbian inns, except in a service capacity. Now, as he groped among the close dark shapes of these buildings he found himself wondering how he could check on whoever might be in them, without raising some kind of alarm.

Just then he caught sight of a thin blade of yellow light between two hide curtains of a building around the corner from one he had just passed. He turned and went toward the light; but as he passed by a little patch of deeper shadow a hand reached out and took him by the arm.

"Do you *want* to get killed?" hissed a voice.

And of course, it spoke Basic. For both the hand and voice were human.

CHAPTER   11

THE grip on John's arm drew him away, deeper into the shadow and around behind a building that blocked him off from the window light. They came on a door of this building and John felt himself led through its hide curtain. In the utter blackness of the interior, the hand left his arm. John stopped, instinctively; completely lost in the leather-smelling obscurity. Then there was a scratch, a sputter, and a candle burst into light only a few feet from him, blinding him.

John blinked helplessly for several seconds against the sudden illumination. Gradually he became able to see again, and when he did, he found himself looking down—for the first time in two days—into the face of one of the prettiest young women he had seen in a long time.

She was perhaps half a foot shorter than he was, but at first glance looked taller by reason of her slimness and the tailored coveralls she wore. To John's Dilbian-accustomed eyes, she looked tiny, not to say fragile. Her chestnut hair swept in two wide wings back on each side of her head. Her eyes were green-blue above marked cheekbones that gave her a sculptured look. Her nose was a thin, her lips firm rather than full, and her small chin had a determined shape.

John blinked again.

"Who—?" he managed, after a minute.

"I'm Ty Lamorc," she said. "Keep your voice down!"

"Ty Lamorc?"

"Yes."

"Are you sure?" stammered John. "I mean, you—"

"Who were you expecting to run into away out here in the center of—oh, I know!" she glared at him. "It's that Greasy Face name the Dilbians gave me. You were expecting some sort of witch."

"Certainly not," said John.

"Well, for your information, they just happened to see me putting on makeup one day."

"Oh."

"That's where the name came from."

"Oh, of course. I never thought—"

"I'll bet you didn't."

"Really," said John.

"Anyway, never mind that now. The point is, what on Earth are you doing out here? Do you want to get knocked on the head?"

"I was trying to find One Man—" John suddenly stiffened and lowered his voice. "Is the Terror back here?"

"No, but Boy Is She Built is. She's been guarding me. And she'll kill you if she gets her hands on you. She hasn't even told the Terror you're after him."

John stared.

"I don't understand," he said.

"The Terror wouldn't run from a fight. He'd run toward it. He thinks it's just the Hill Bluffer after him with a demand from the Humrog mayor that he bring me back. Boy Is She Built doesn't want the Terror to get into trouble by killing you."

"But she's willing to do it, herself."

"She's in love with the Terror. That's the way she thinks. And she doesn't know—well, how essentially harmless your mission is. Now, what we've got to do is smuggle you back into the dormitory before she catches you. She won't go in there after you. It's treaty ground inside, anyway."

"Hold on a minute," said John, as Ty took hold of his arm again. He did not move. "Aren't we getting this a little mixed up? I mean—who's rescuing who? I came along here to find you and bring you back to Humrog. Well, I've found you. Come along back to the main inn building with me and I'll wake up the Hill Bluffer and explain things—"

"You don't," interrupted Ty with feeling, "understand a blasted thing about these Dilbians, Half-Pint —I mean, Mr. Tardy."

"Call me John," said John.

"John, you just don't understand the situation. The Terror left me here because he knew Boy Is She Built would stay on watch. And she will. She'll be back looking for me in ten more minutes; and if I'm not where she left me, she'll be right after us. So even if we did try to get away, she'd catch us. Also, the Bluffer's honor bound to deliver you to the Terror. The Terror's honor bound to fight you when that happens, or any time he finds out you're after him to take me away. So he'd be after us, too. And if she couldn't catch us, *he* certainly could."

"But—"

"Will you listen to me?" hissed Ty. "I'm a sociologist. I've put in six months studying these people.

What we've got to do is keep you out of danger until
the Terror takes me into the Hollows, his own clan
territory. Once he does that, it'll be up to the grandfathers of his clan to decide what happens to me, and
you and the Terror, and all. I can demand a hearing
and explain that I've got no connection by blood or
anything like that with Joshua, and then they'll rule
that the Terror wasn't within his rights to steal me in
retaliation for Joshua's insult; I'm sure they will.
Then, they'll be no reason for the Terror to fight you
and we can both go back, safely."

"If you're so sure of that," said John, "how come
I was sent out here in the first place?"

"Oh, Joshua doesn't understand these people much
better than you do."

"I can believe that," said John.

"So, you go back to the main inn building now.
And be careful!"

"Well . . ." John hesitated. "I still think I ought to
play safe and try to take you away, tonight. With a
good start and by wrecking the Knobby Gorge bridge
—" He paused and considered her. She was *re-
markably* small and fragile-looking. The thought of
the Terror grabbing her up and running off with her
made him growl a little bit inside, at that. "I just don't
think we should take any chances with your safety,"
he wound up.

Ty Lamorc stood perfectly still for a long second,
looking at him. The expression on her face was one he
could not fathom.

"Well, John!" she said, finally, and suddenly her
eyes were quite soft. She reached out and touched his
arm. "That was very nice of you," she said, in a low
voice. "Thank you, John."

Then, suddenly, before he could move, she blew out the candle. In the sudden darkness he heard the hide curtain flap and sway.

"Ty?" he said.

But there was no answer. She had gone.

He felt his way out of the hut, and emerged into the dimness of the starlit night outside. He squinted around himself, located the main building and headed through the darkness toward it.

Something large and leathery descended out of nowhere, wrapping around him. A couple of powerful arms lifted him off the ground. He fought, but it was useless. He felt himself being carried off.

Inside the tight folds of the leather enfolding him he began to suffocate. Very shortly, he lost consciousness. Things became soft and pillowy about him. He seemed to swim off into blackness.

Then, there was nothing.

CHAPTER   12

JOHN awoke with the vague impression that he had overslept on a work day and was due on the job. Opening his eyes, he was puzzled and surprised to see the intricate branches of treetops black against the paling grey of a predawn sky.

How did he get here? he wondered.

His next vague impression was that he had been someplace and drunk too much the night before. He had the ugly taste in his mouth and dull skullcap of a headache that goes with a hangover. Then everything to do with Dilbia came back to his mind with a rush, up to and including the memory of being carried off after leaving his talk with Ty Lamorc.

He sat up to look around him, achieving this with a difficulty that led him to discover that his forearms and ankles were bound and tied with thick rope.

He found he was seated on damp leaves over damp forest earth, in a little clearing. A small fire was burning about fifteen feet from him. At the fire sat Boy Is She Built and the short, broad Hemnoid, Tark-*ay*.

Boy Is She Built jerked up her head to look as John raised himself into a sitting position, and Tark-*ay's* glance followed in a more leisurely manner. In the wild woods, sitting over the pale fire just as dawn was breaking in the sky, they looked like a scene out of some oriental book of legends, the wise man and the beast. Just then Boy Is She Built opened her mouth and blew the illusion to smithereens.

"He's conscious!" she said. The tone of her voice was accusing.

"To be sure, little lady," responded Tark-*ay*. His voice, like the voice of all Hemnoids, had a heavy, liquid quality. It was somewhat higher in tone than that of a male Dilbian would have been. In fact, he and Boy Is She Built operated in about the same vocal range. "He's been merely asleep for several hours now. I was very careful."

"In the old days," said Boy Is She Built, hopefully, "they used to break the legs of prisoners to keep them from getting away."

"We aren't barbarians, after all though, little lady," protested Tark-*ay* mildly.

"Oh, you're all so stubborn!" said Boy Is She Built, huffily. "It isn't good enough just to hit him over the head. Oh, no! We have to carry him here, and carry him there. My Terror's not like that."

"That," pointed out Tark-*ay*, "is exactly why we don't want your Terror to know this little fellow is after him. If I might remind you—"

"Well, I'm getting tired of waiting, that's all!" said Boy Is She Built. "If the Beer-Guts Bouncer isn't here by an hour after sunrise, I'm going to hit him on the head, and that's that."

"I would have to stop you from doing anything like that, little lady."

"You wouldn't dare!" She glared at him. "I'd tell the Terror!"

"That would be too bad, little lady. But," said Tark-*ay* almost apologetically, "you ought to understand that I would still have to stop you. It would be my duty. And you should also understand that in the regrettable instance of the Terror and I coming to blows, I would have no doubt of emerging the winner."

"You! I can just see you beating up the Terror!" said Boy Is She Built and laughed nastily. "He's twice as big as you are."

"Not twice. Somewhat taller, it's true. But our weights aren't so far apart as most of your people might think. And besides, it would make no real difference—even if Streamside was, in truth, twice my size."

"Why not, smarty?" said Boy Is She Built.

"Because of the high skills and arts of unarmed combat, developed on my world, in which I am an expert. Now, suppose Streamside should rush at me with intent to do me harm."

"He'd swarm all over you."

"Not at all." Tark-*ay* got to his feet in one quick motion. "He comes rushing at me. I meet him, so—!" Suddenly, the short Hemnoid twisted, half bent over, and lashed out with a foot. "Then, before he can recover, I am all over *him!*" Tark-*ay* straightened up and bounded forward. His open hand made slashing cutting motions in the air.

"You aren't going to stop the Terror by *slapping* him," said Boy Is She Built. "Oh yes, I can just see you slapping my Terror!"

"Slapping?" said Tark-*ay*. There was a fair-sized length of log near the fire. Tark-*ay* picked it up and leaned it against a close tree. His open hand cut at it, and the log broke loudly into two sections. "You will be happier, little lady," said Tark-*ay* sitting down once more by the fire, "if your Terror never has anything to do with me in an unfriendly way."

He bent to put one of the broken log-pieces on the fire. And John, watching, saw a peculiar glitter in the eyes of Boy Is She Built, as she gazed at the Hemnoid. One furry hand of the young Dilbian female reached for a large rock nearby, hesitated, and then returned to her lap. It occurred to John that Tark-*ay* might be an expert in the high skills and arts of unarmed combat developed on his world; but he was pretty much of a numbskull when it came to female psychology. Boy Is She Built had been going to a good deal of trouble to dispose of John because she thought of him as a threat to Streamside. And now Tark-*ay* had just incautiously revealed that he was also a threat, not only to the Terror's honor, but to his very life and limb.

Of course, a loyal female should perhaps have laughed the matter off, scorning to doubt her husband-to-be. But Boy Is She Built, while loyal enough to suit almost anybody, appeared to have a strong practical streak in her nature as well.

John licked his lips, which were very dry.

"I could use a drink of water," he said out loud.

Boy Is She Built looked up the slope at him.

"Hmph!" said Boy Is She Built. She did not stir.

"Are we barbarians?" cried Tark-*ay*, bouncing to his feet. He went to a canteen hanging from a nearby limb of a tree, brought it to John, unscrewed the top, peeled off a sterile cup, filled it and held it to John's lips while he drank.

"How about loosening these ropes?" asked John, after he had gulped a couple of cups of the water.

"I'm sorry. Very sorry," said Tark-*ay* and returned to the fireside.

They all sat in silence, for some little while during which the sky turned pink and the local sun shoved his upper rim into sight behind the surrounding trees. Tark-*ay* got to his feet and began to bounce up and down and down, clapping his hands over his head. John stared. So did Boy Is She Built.

"What's wrong?" cried Boy Is She Built.

"Nothing, little lady," replied Tark-*ay,* "merely my exercises which I do periodically during the morning hours."

"Well, I thought you'd eaten something!" said Boy Is She Built. She relaxed again. "Or sat on a splinter. Or something."

Tark-*ay* abandoned his initial exercise. He began one in which he leaped up from the ground, clicked his heels, clasped his hands, and winked. As soon as he hit ground, he bounced up and went through the whole process all over again.

"That's the most ridiculous thing I ever saw," said Boy Is She Built. "What do you do something like that for?"

"It is part of my training, little lady," gasped Tark-*ay*. "A true master of the skills and arts does it once each time before he says anything. It builds character."

"Well, I think it's utterly ridiculous," said Boy Is She Built. She lay down and curled up on her side. "Call me when the Beer-Guts Bouncer gets here. I'm going to take a little nap."

She closed her eyes. Tark-*ay* continued bouncing. He ran through several more exercises before he ran down. Then, wiping his forehead, he waddled over and sat down by John.

"She is a trial, that little lady," he said, nodding at Boy Is She Built.

"Oh?" said John, wondering if this was leading up to something.

"Yes. Irrepressible youth. The eternal juvenile young female whose world is completely oriented to her own parochial ego. Anything that does not fit her own image of the universe is dismissed as unworthy of consideration."

"Is that so?" said John.

"Only too truly so. You come from a civilized race the way I do. You understand me. She's driving me crazy."

"How?"

"She's just so—impossible. She knows nothing. And she thinks she knows everything. I was trying to explain a chance remark I made the other day about psychological pressure. Now, *you* know as well as I do she knows nothing about psychology."

"I wouldn't think so," said John.

"How could she? On this barbaric world? I started to explain what psychology was, to explain my remark. Well, first she got angry and said she knew as much about it as I did."

John was getting interested in spite of the ropes and the situation.

"What did you say to that?" he asked.

"I pointed out that this couldn't be true, since there were no colleges upon her world where she could have learned it."

"That stopped her?"

"No," said Tark-*ay* sadly. "She said, there was, too. She had studied all about psychology at the college at Blunder Bush."

"Blunder Bush?"

"There's no such place," said Tark-*ay*, "of course. I told her this, and she claimed that I just didn't know about it. That it was highly secret. It must have been plain to her that I was seeing through all this, so she went on, piling her fictions higher. Her whole family were college graduates, she told me. She had been offered a teaching position herself. She wound up telling me that the Streamside Terror was actually an instructor at his college; and all his running around and fighting was just so people wouldn't suspect his true abilities. Well, well—"

Tark-*ay* sighed heavily, got up, and went back to the fire.

John frowned. He had been expecting the Hemnoid to get even more confidential, and had even hoped he could find some lever in the conversation which he might turn to his own advantage in getting out of this fix. But Tark-*ay* had broken things off too abruptly.

John could have sworn Tark-*ay* had settled down beside him with intentions for an extended conversation. What had made the short Hemnoid change his mind?

Then John heard the distant crackling of footfalls among the dry leaves under the trees a little distance off. They were approaching behind John, and he found he was too tightly trussed to turn around. At the fire, Tark-*ay* busied himself breaking up small pieces of wood and adding them to the blaze. He did not look up.

The footfalls approached. They came right up behind John and stopped. John heard the slow, even sound of deep breathing, above and behind his head.

Then the feet moved whoever it was around in front of John and he saw a great yellow moon-face beaming down at him from eight feet above the ground.

"Well, well," said a heavy, liquid voice, "so, here's

our quarry, trussed and ready for roasting. How should we season him, Tark-*ay*?"

It was the Hemnoid ambassador to Dilbia, Gulark-*ay*.

CHAPTER 13

"YOU'LL think of something, Mr. Ambassador, I'm sure," replied Tark-*ay* and the two Hemnoids chuckled together like a couple of gallon jugs of machine oil being poured out on the ground.

The sound woke Boy Is She Built. She sat up.

"Here you are!" she said to Gulark-*ay*.

"Absolutely right, Boy Is She Built," replied the Hemnoid ambassador. "Here, indeed, I am. You don't look pleased?"

"I don't know why we had to wait for you," she said.

"Because," said Gulark-*ay*, "there's more to this than simply throwing someone you don't like over a cliff. Remember? You were only supposed to take his wrist radio there at Brittle Rock, not drop him into a five hundred foot canyon."

"It would have saved a lot of trouble," said Boy Is She Built. She looked rebellious.

"So you think. But, as you would have found out, if you'd been successful, what it actually would have done would have been to cause a lot of trouble. Do you think the Shorty authorities are going to let one of their people get killed here on your world and not want to know what happened?"

"They wouldn't dare make a fuss," said Boy Is She

Built. "They need to make friends with us real people. Just like you Fatties do. If they attacked us, you'd just like the excuse to back us up." She snorted. A curiously feminine version of the Hill Bluffer's favorite emotional outlet. "They wouldn't dare make trouble over one little Shorty."

"Never mind," said Gulark-*ay*. "Life's a little more complicated than you think, Boy Is She Built. You don't get things without paying for them. And, believe me, you can't just kill a Shorty on a whim without paying for that, either."

"Oh, you sound just like my father!" said Boy Is She Built, furiously.

"Thank you," said Gulark-*ay*, dryly. He turned away from her and sat down by John on the ground, spreading his robes over his enormous knees.

"And how is our cat's-paw doing?" he asked.

"You're talking to me?" said John.

"Of course," said Gulark-*ay*. "Didn't you realize that's what you've been all along?"

"To tell you the truth," said John, "and now that you ask me, no, I didn't."

"Such trust," said Gulark-*ay*.

"And faith," said John. "To say nothing of experience." He pointed out something. "I'm a little bit older and more widely traveled than Boy Is She Built, for example."

"What's he saying about me?" said Boy Is She Built, lifting her head up. "What's travel got to do with it?"

"But I'm only telling you what's true," said Gulark-*ay*, bassly and liquidly. "How do you think Tark-*ay* here, and Boy Is She Built happened to be waiting for you on the trail your first day out? How do you think Boy Is She Built happened to know enough to deprive you of your wrist phone?"

"Now, that's an interesting point," said John. "You say she took my wrist phone off. Why? When she was going to throw me over the cliff, anyway?"

"She wasn't supposed to do anything but get the wrist phone," said Gulark-*ay*. "As to why she still bothered to do that after deciding to kill you, is something you'd have to ask her."

"They told me to," said Boy Is She Built sulkily.

"But you miss the point," said Gulark-*ay* to John, "which is how we knew where you were going to be and when. Aren't you going to ask me who tipped off Boy Is She Built?"

"You did."

"Not at all. Your ambassador, Joshua."

John looked at him sourly.

"You expect me to believe that, don't you?"

"Why not?" Gulark-*ay* spread his enormous hands.

"For one reason, because you wouldn't have any reason for telling it to me unless to convince me of something that wasn't true."

"Not at all," said Gulark-*ay*. "Don't you know about us Hemnoids? We're a cruel people. We enjoy seeing others suffer. I enjoy dashing your faith in Joshua Guy—particularly because I've no doubt in the back of your mind, you've been planning on using action by him, in the event of your death, as a threat to make me let you go."

John had. But he kept his face bland.

"Seems to me," he said, "you protest your cruelty too much."

Gulark-*ay* shook his head. He seemed to be quite

earnest and enjoying the conversation.

"That's because," he said, "according to your mores it is immoral to make someone else suffer. But according to my mores it is not only moral, but eminently respectable. It is a skill, a high art."

"Do you jump up in the air and click your heels before beginning?" asked John, sourly.

For the first time, Gulark-*ay* looked slightly baffled. Tark-*ay*, busily poking at the fire with his head down, did not offer to interpret the remark for his ambassador.

"We seem to be drifting off the subject," said Gulark-*ay*. "The point I am laboring to get across to you is that your Joshua Guy is to be no help to you. He had you written off from the beginning."

"Are you sure you aren't judging according to Hemnoid mores?" said John. "Human ambassadors usually operate a little differently."

"No doubt, no doubt," said Gulark-*ay* chuckling richly. "But there are special reasons in the case of Mr. Guy. You're a draftee, aren't you, my friend?"

"That's right," said John. "A willing draftee, I might point out."

"No doubt, no doubt," said Gulark-*ay* chuckling richly, and chuckled again. "Well, so is your ambassador to Dilbia."

"Guy? Drafted?"

John blinked in spite of himself. There was, of course, no technical reason why you couldn't draft a man with the proper talents into a diplomatic post. It was just kind of farfetched, that was all.

"Quite right," said Gulark-*ay*. "Joshua Guy, three years ago, had retired after a full lifetime in the diplomatic service. He was planning to spend the rest of his life cultivating certain species of your native flora—I don't remember just what. Roses, or some such name. However, his government thought they needed him on Dilbia, and so here they sent him here."

John accepted this in silence, without arguing or accepting. But he was busy thinking.

"Of course," went on Gulark-*ay*,—and he did, indeed, seem to be enjoying himself— "Joshua has been very eager all this time to get relieved of his duties and be allowed to return to his roses, or his turnips, or whatever. And of course you realize, the only way for anyone like him to get relieved would be to—how do you put it?—goof up so badly that he would have to be replaced. He fomented this whole fuss with Boy Is She Built just to create the proper kind of trouble."

"In that case he didn't need me," said John. "Ty Lamorc being kidnaped by the Terror was trouble enough."

"Ah, yes, but you see, he found he had misplayed his hand in the case of Ty. That young female was sent out here by a different branch of your government. One which would be only to glad to pin something on the Diplomatic Service. If anything happened to Ty, it began to look as if Joshua might face not merely retirement; but trial for manslaughter, or worse. On the other hand, by throwing you to the Terror, he could more or less ransom Ty. And an obscure young biochemist with no connections could be spared with only the routine amount of reprimand and investigation."

"Very interesting," said John. "And you undertook to mess up Guy's plans just out of your natural, healthy instinct for cruelty? Tell me another fairy tale."

"You misjudge me!" said Gulark-*ay* sharply. "I

have my personal pride and pleasures; but first and foremost, I am a servant and representative of my people. It's as important to our plans as to the plans of you humans, to get the inside track on friendship with the Dilbians. A bad and an unwilling human ambassador such as Guy is just what we're pleased to see on Dilbia. It was my duty to back up Guy's superiors in this matter and see that he failed in trying to arrange for his own retirement."

"Well, then," said John. "Since we're all working together in this, why don't you just cut these ropes off; and we can all go back to Sour Ford Inn for breakfast."

Gurlark-*ay* quivered and shook with sudden laughter. His laughing was so infectious that shortly Tark-*ay* and Boy Is She Built had joined in the humor. And John, to his own surprise, had to fight back the beginnings of a smile.

"Well, now!" chortled Gulark-*ay*, running down at last. "If that doesn't—! Let you go! We couldn't do that, Mr. Tardy. You see, you're the price of Boy Is She Built's assistance. She wants you out of the way, permanently. We promised this; and she promised to talk the Terror into giving Miss Lamorc up without argument, when his clan grandfathers order him to do so." He looked at John. "Which," he said, delicately, "they will undoubtedly do when you are found dead within their clan territory of the Hollows, just over the river."

John looked at Gulark-*ay*, gave a short incredulous laugh and looked away.

"Good! Very good, Mr. Tardy!" cried Gulark-*ay* bursting into a fresh gallon-jug's worth of laughter. "Oh, it's going to be a pleasure to work on you, Mr.

Tardy, when we get down to actual business. Well—" he heaved himself erect and went over to sit down by Tark-*ay* and Boy Is She Built at the fire.

"Well!" he said again, clapping his big hands together, briskly. "I don't believe in being a hog about these things. All good suggestions are welcome. How'll we do it?"

"If you don't mind, Mr. Ambassador," said Tark-*ay,* with polite eagerness. "There's a new technique my cousin was reading about recently. He wrote me about it in his last letter. A sort of peeling-back of the fingernails."

"Well now, that sounds interesting," said Gulark-*ay.* "I'm no expert, more's the pity on human nerve-endings, particularly in the fingertip areas; but we can assume a basic similarity. We'll put that on the list. Now, I myself, have a small specialty involving the inside of the mouth, if no one objects?" He looked at the other two.

"Why don't we just hit him over the head?" said Boy Is She Built.

Tark-*ay* gave her a look of scorn.

"We aren't barbarians!" he said.

CHAPTER 14

THE discussion went on in lively fashion for some time. And an amazing thing happened to John. He dozed off. The subject matter might have been enough to keep him awake; but the two Hemnoids had become unintelligibly technical; and the tone had become the tone of in-group discussions the universe over. Half the wrangling was over authorities and precedents, rather than about the actual performance contemplated. Moreover, John had had two rough nights and days in a row. His body made up his mind for him. It went to sleep.

When he reawakened, the sun was well up over the trees, and he found that he was not the only one who had become tired of the discussion. Boy Is She Built was reading the two Hemnoids the riot act.

"—and I think you're disgusting, both of you!" she was informing them, in anything but well-modulated tones. "And crazy! And stupid! I keep telling you why don't you just hit him over the head? But, oh no! Not you! It's got to be first we'll do this. And then we'll do that! And then—oh, no, we can't do that, because it's finish him off too quick—or somebody else tried it and it didn't work out too well."

"Little lady," began Tark-*ay*.

"You give me a pain!" cried Boy Is She Built.

"And you aren't even *mad* at him, that's what gets me! If it wasn't for Streamside, I don't think I'd even let you have him! You're just—just—you're disgusting, both of you!"

"You don't understand," said Gulark-*ay*. "The point is—"

"Well, I'm glad I don't. If this is the way you Hemnoids are, I'm not sure I don't like Shorties better, after all. I'll bet if it was *him* helping me and you two tied up over there, he'd tell me to go right ahead and hit you over the head. He wouldn't go on arguing about doing this first, and doing that second." Boy Is She Built made an unsuccessful effort to imitate the deep liquidity of the Hemnoid voices gloating over a particularly attractive idea, " 'and we moost try thees. Oh, wee surleee moost!' You both give me a pain!"

Tark-*ay*, glancing helplessly away from her, found his glance meeting that of John's; and shrugged helplessly at the human.

"Well," said Gulark-*ay*, shaking his head and getting to his feet, "there's no help for it. We'd just be wasting him to get to work now. I have to get on to see the grandfathers of the Hollows clan; and I can't get back until late afternoon, now. Let's put it all off until this evening. I'll bring some supplies from my stuff, when I get back, something good in the way of food and drink, and we can make a bang-up night of it. How does that strike you, Tark-*ay?*"

"Mr. Ambassador," said Tark-*ay*, his voice full of deep emotion, "you are a gentleman!"

"Thank you, thank you indeed," said Gulark-*ay*. "Well, I'm on my way, then. Traveling in my direction, Boy Is She Built?"

"I should think so!" Boy Is She Built jumped to her feet. "I was supposed to meet Streamside just two hours after the sun was up, and I forgot all about it. He gets awfully impatient. Maybe he went off and left that Shorty female alone."

And without even waiting for Gulark-*ay,* Boy Is She Built hurried off.

"Mr. Ambassador," said Tark-*ay,* looking after her. "You don't know. You just don't know."

"Cheer up," said Gulark-*ay.* "It'll be all remembered to your advantage in my reports." He rearranged his robes. "I'll be back this evening, then."

"May the hours fly until then, Mr. Ambassador."

"Indeed," said Gulark-*ay;* and departed in his turn.

Tark-*ay* left alone with John, sighed heavily. He produced a curved knife from his robe, with which he proceeded to clean his fingernails, meanwhile heaving another occasional heavy sigh. Finished, he stuck the knife into a piece of firewood beside him and tapped its hilt with his finger to make it vibrate back and forth. After a while he gave even this up. His eyes closed. He dozed.

John, lying still, watched the Hemnoid carefully from fifteen feet of distance. It had not occurred to John before, but Tark-*ay* had probably not had a good night's sleep either for some time. He waited.

Tark-*ay* slid down the tree against which he was leaning. He began to breathe heavily with a whistling overtone which John took to be the Hemnoid equivalent of a snore. He lay sprawled out. John's eyes went to the knife, still stuck in the chunk of firewood.

As quietly as he could, John slid down flat on the

ground himself. Luckily, it was downhill. He rolled over once. Twigs crackled and pebbles rattled away from him. But Tark-*ay* did not wake up. John rolled over a second time.

Three minutes later he was rubbing his bound wrists against the blade of the upright knife blade. It was not as easy as it looked in the pictures John had seen. He did a pretty good job of slicing up his wrists in the process, and the rope was thick. Also, he discovered, it is not easy to get pressure against the blade of a knife stuck upright in a piece of wood. The angle is all wrong.

Nevertheless, some ten minutes after he had first started his roll downhill, he was cutting his feet loose from their bindings, knife in hand. He got the foot-tyings parted, stuck the knife in his belt and took off, as quietly as he could up the slope into the trees.

Tark-*ay* had not stirred.

John was just about to congratulate himself on having gained his freedom without mishap, when an infuriated roar behind him stopped him in his tracks. Instinctively, he dodged behind a nearby tree, turned and looked back.

A Dilbian with coal-black fur was just charging into the clearing John had just left, forty feet below. Tark-*ay* was scrambling to his feet.

"Where is he?" roared this Dilbian. "Point him out!"

"What are you doing here?" said Tark-*ay*.

"Don't try to pretend you don't know. I found out! When Boy Is She Built didn't come back in time, I went looking for her. When I found her coming out of these woods she had some explaining to do. I know it all now. Where's this Shorty who's been acting as if I was running away from him?"

"You're too late," said Tark-*ay*, not without a certain tone of satisfaction in his voice, it seemed to John. "He's escaped." And he pointed to the cut sections of the rope that had bound John.

"Escaped?" The Dilbian, who could be no other than the Streamside Terror, had gone ominously quiet. John, peering at the two of them from around the tree, was trying to make up his mind whether to make a run for it, or lie quiet and hope they would not come searching this way.

He decided to lie quiet. It would give him a chance to case the Streamside Terror and see, if possible, what gave that Dilbian his reputation as a battler. So far, there had been no indications. The Terror was by no means the biggest Dilbian John had seen; he was considerably shorter, for example, than the Hill Bluffer. Perhaps his unusualness was a matter of reflexes.

"You let him escape?" said the Terror, mildly.

"Alas," said Tark-*ay*, a trifle smugly.

"WHY?" roared the Terror.

Hemnoids were no more without nerves than humans, apparently. Tark-*ay* jumped involuntarily, as the Terror erupted with full lung power two feet from his nose.

"That's not for you to question!" snapped Tark-*ay*. "And furthermore—"

There was no furthermore. For just then, the Terror lit into him.

Note: noted John. Terror gives no warning. Does not telegraph punches.

The fight became active in the clearing below John. Tark-*ay* was valiantly attempting to employ his high skills and arts; but seemed somewhat hampered by the fact that the Terror had closed with him immediately and they were both now rolling around on the ground together.

Note: noted John. When no stream available, Terror attempts to batter opponent against handy rocks and trees.

No matter how you sliced it, the battle proceeding below was an awe-inspiring bit of action. The combined weight of the two opponents must have run close to fifteen hundred pounds; both were skilled fighters, and both in top condition.

Note: noted John. Liberal use of nails and teeth gives Terror considerable advantage over opponent not trained to this sort of fighting and not expecting same.

The Terror was definitely gaining the upper hand. Tark-*ay* seemed to be weakening.

Note: noted John. Terror particularly quick for someone so large. Would smallness of human and consequent greater maneuverability of human give human slight advantage in this department however? Possibly. But what good would it do just to keep dodging?

The fight below seemed drawing to its close with the Terror emerging as a clear winner. John suddenly realized that with all this noise going on, now was the ideal time for him to get away from the vicinity and travel.

He traveled.

At first, he merely headed off through the woods in a plain and simple attempt to put as much distance between himself and the place of his recent captivity, as possible.

As soon as he had covered about a quarter mile or

so, his first urgency dwindled a bit. He took time out to get a handkerchief out of his pocket, tear it in half and bind up the cuts on his wrists, which had been bleeding somewhat messily, all down his hands. There was no water nearby in which he could wash his hands, but he rubbed them in dry leaves, and got them looking better than they had before.

Then he sat down on a fallen tree to catch his breath and began to think about getting his bearings.

He had no idea in what direction he had been carried the night before after being wrapped up in the leather blanket, or whatever it was that had been used to bundle him up. However, he remembered Gulark-*ay*'s reference to Clan Hollows territory, "just over the river"; and he recalled that Sour Ford Inn had been right at a river. Consequently, the river in question could not be far from him; and once he found it, he could go up or down it until he found Sour Ford and the Bluffer.

John utilized some elementary woodcraft. He hunted for the tallest tree he could find close at hand and climbed it.

From its top he spotted the river, about half a mile away and almost due west according to the sun. And on this side of the river, a mile or two upstream was some cluster of buildings which was probably Sour Ford Inn.

John climbed down again and headed west, not forgetting to keep his eyes peeled for the Terror or even for Tark-*ay*, assuming the Hemnoid had been left in condition to travel.

However, he met no one. When he reached the river, he found there was a trail running alongside it; and he had hardly proceeded half a mile up the trail before he ran into a group of five Dilbians.

"Hey! Whoop!" hollered the first of these, the minute he got around a bend in the trail and spotted John. "There he is! Where'd you run off to, Shorty? The Bluffer's got half the people between here and Twin Peaks out looking for you!"

CHAPTER   15

"NEVER," said the Bluffer, as he swung through the forest with John on his back, "again. Nothing with legs. If it's got legs it can deliver itself. The mail's for things that can't get around on its own. That's what the mail's for."

John felt too comfortable to be disturbed by the postman's grousing. He had put his foot down for the first time, when the group he had run into had brought him back to the inn, and insisted on a couple of hours sleep in ordinary fashion. He had gotten them, in the peace of the inn dormitory. When he had woken up, he had decided as well to quit worrying about possible allergies and have something more than paste and pill concentrates to eat.

He had stuffed himself, accordingly. Dilbian bread, he discovered was coarse and full of uncompletely milled kernels, the cheese was sour and the meat tough, with a sour taste to it. It tasted delicious, and he just wished he had been able to hold a bit more. No allergic reactions had showed up so far; and now, with a full stomach, he drowsed on the back of the Dilbian postman, all but falling asleep in the saddle. As he drowsed, he wondered dreamily about his escape from Tark-*ay*. It all seemed almost too good to be true.

They were descending now into a country of lower altitudes, although they were still far above the central plains of this particular Dilbian continent. The central plains, being warmer in the summer than the Dilbians liked, were only sparsely settled. They regarded them as lush, unhealthy places where a man from the uplands lost his moral fiber quickly and fell into unnamed vices. Black sheep from the respectable communities of the clans often ended up down there, where the living was easy and no questions asked about a man's past.

So, the higher Hollows area was regarded as lowlands, in the ordinary sense by the mountain-living Dilbians. And in fact, John noticed that the countryside here did look a lot different. A new type of tree, something like a birch, was now to be seen among the hitherto unbroken ranks of sprucelike coniferoids of the uplands. And fern and brush began to put in an appearance.

All this could have been quite interesting to John if he had not been half-asleep; and if he had not had other things swimming about in the back of his mind, specifically, that apparently unavoidable meeting with the Streamside Terror, to which events and the Hill Bluffer seemed to be rushing him in spite of himself.

He felt like someone who has been caught in an avalanche, and now was riding it down the mountainside—for the moment on top of the moving mass, but with an inevitable cliff edge looming ahead. What the blazes was he to do, he wondered dully out of his half-awake state, when he found himself suddenly shoved, barehanded against the Terror? Doubtless with an impenetrable ring of Dilbian spectators hemming them both in, as well.

And for what? Why? Everybody from Joshua on through Gulark-*ay* seemed to have a different explanation of the reasons for the combat taking place. Everybody's patsy, that's what I am, thought John gloomily and dozed off again. Time went by.

He awoke suddenly. The Hill Bluffer had stopped unexpectedly, with a startled grunt. John sat up and looked around with the uncertainty of a man still fogged by sleep.

They were out of the woods. They had emerged into a small valley in which a cluster of buildings stood in the brown color of their peeled, and naturally weathered logs, haphazardly about a stream that ran the valley's length. Beyond the village, or whatever it was, there was a short of natural amphitheater made by a curved indentation in the far rock wall of the valley. Past this, the path curved on through an opening in the valley wall and into further forest.

However, it was not this pleasant little village scene that caught John's attention as he came fully awake.

It was a group of five brawny Dilbians who stood squarely athwart the path before himself and the Bluffer.

Armed with axes.

The Hill Bluffer had not said a word from the moment of John's awakening. Now he exploded. In his outrage he was almost incoherent.

"You—you—" he stuttered, roaringly. "You got the almighty nerve—you got the *guts*—! You dare stop the mail? Who do you think—just *who* is it thinks he's got the right—"

"Clan Hollows in full meeting, that's who," said the middle axman, a Dilbian almost as tall as the

Bluffer, himself. "Come on with us."

The Bluffer took two steps backwards and hunched his shoulders. John felt himself lifted on the swell of the postman's big back muscles.

"Let's just see you take us!" snarled the postman. He sounded slightly berserk. Up on his back, John swallowed automatically looking at the Dilbian axes. John was in rather the same position as someone with a drunken or excitable friend who is in the process of getting them both into a fight. Harnessed to the Bluffer the way he was, there was no way he could quickly get down and loose in the case of trouble; and just at the moment the Bluffer did not seem to be thinking of taking time out to put his mail in a safe place before committing suicide.

"Hey!" said John, tapping the Bluffer on the shoulder. He might as well have tapped one of the Dilbian mountains in a like manner, for all the attention he attracted.

"Spread out, boys," said the head axman, hefting his forty-pound tool-weapon. The line began to extend at either end and curve in to flank the Bluffer. "Postman, officially in the name of Clan Hollows, I'm bidding you to immediate meeting. The grandfathers are waiting for you there, postman. And that Shorty you got with you."

The Hill Bluffer ground his teeth together. Seated just back of the Dilbian's mandible hinges the way John was, it made an awesome sound.

"He's mine." The postman sounded like he was talking through clenched jaws. "Until delivered! Come try take him, you hollow-scuttling, thieving low-land loopers, you Clan Hollows sons of—"

The axman were beginning to snarl and look red-eyed in turn. Desperate times, thought John, call for desperate measures.

He leaned forward, got the Bluffer's right ear firmly in his teeth. And bit.

"Yii!" roared the Bluffer—and spun about, almost snapping John's head off at the neck. "Who did that—? Oh! What're you trying to pull, Half-Pint." He tried to twist his neck around and look John in the face.

"That's right," said John. "Get in a fight! Get the government mail damaged! Back on my Shorty world they've got better postmen than that."

"They can't do this to me," rumbled the Bluffer, but his voice had noticeably dropped in volume.

"Sure," said John. "Your honor. But duty comes before honor. How about me? It's as much against my honor to let these axmen take me in. There's nothing *I'd* like better," said John, smiling falsely, "than to get down from your back here and help you take these Hollows unmentionables to pieces. But do I think of myself? No. I—"

"Listen at him," said one of the axmen. "Help take us to pieces! Hor, hor."

"You think that's funny, do you!" flared the Bluffer afresh, spinning to face the tickled axman. "You just remember this is the Shorty chasing down the Terror. How'd you like to tangle with the Terror, yourself, hairy-legs?"

"Huh!" said the other, losing his good humor suddenly, and hefting his ax. However, he did throw a second look over the Bluffer's shoulder at John and stood where he was.

"All right, men," said the leader of the axmen. "Enough of this chit-chat! When I give the word—"

"Cut it! Cut it!" boomed the Bluffer. "We'll go with you. Half-Pint's right. Lucky for you."

"Huh!" said the axman who had laughed before. But as they all fell into a sort of hollow square with the Bluffer and John in the middle, he stayed well to the rear. Together they marched down into the valley and toward the amphitheater at the far end.

They went through the village, which under the bright early afternoon sun seemed to have a fiesta air about it, and to the amphitheater. The main road up which they traveled was alive with Dilbians of all ages moving in the same direction and many questions were thrown at the guard around John and the Bluffer. The guard, marching stiffly, with axes over their shoulders, looked straight ahead to a Dilbian and refused to answer.

They came at last to a long, meter-high ledge of rock on which five very ancient-looking male Dilbians sat on one low bench. The one on the far right was a skinny oldster who seemed slightly deaf, since as they came up he was cupping one ear with a shaky hand and shouting at the Dilbian next to him to speak up. As the Bluffer and John were brought to a halt before them, John was astonished to notice the number of other familiar faces in the forefront of the gathering. One Man was there, seated on a sort of camp stool. Ty Lamorc and Boy Is She Built stood not far from the giant Dilbian. And Gulark-*ay* and Joshua Guy were flanking old Shaking Knees, who— whether in his capacity as mayor of Humrog, or father to Boy Is She Built—was looking important.

"Hey!" cried John, trying to attract the attention of the little human ambassador.

Joshua Guy looked up, spotted John, and gave him a large smile and a cheery wave of one hand.

"Beautiful day, isn't it?" called the ambassador; he went back to chatting in a friendly manner with Gulark-*ay* and Shaking Knees.

"I can't see him. Where is he? Get him out in the open!" the deaf grandfather on the end of the bench was snapping fretfully.

"Sit here," said an axman. The Bluffer sat down on a bench. John climbed down from the saddle and sat beside him.

"There he is!" said the deaf grandfather. "Why didn't someone point him out to me before. What? Hey? Speak up!"

He was nudged by the grandfather adjoining. The grandfathers conferred, for the most part in low voices. Then they all sat back on their bench, and the central one waggled a finger at the head axman, who stepped out into the open space before the ledge and turned to the crowd.

"Clan Hollows is now meeting in open session!" he shouted. "No fighting! Everybody listen!"

The crowd muttered, grumbled, and took about forty seconds to subside to a passably low level of noise.

"Ahem!" The center grandfather, a heavy Dilbian whose hair was showing the rusty color of age, cleared his throat. "The grandfathers have called this meeting to discuss a matter of Clan honor. In short: is the honor of Clan Hollows involved in the ruckus that one of the Clan Members, the Streamside Terror, has got himself into?"

"Yes!" spoke up Boy Is She Built.

"Who said that?" said the center grandfather.

"She did," said an axman, pointing at Boy Is She Built.

"Keep her quiet," said the grandfather.

"Shut up!" said the axman to Boy Is She Built.

"I apologize for my daughter to Clan Hollows," said Shaking Knees.

"You ought to," said the center Clan Hollows grandfather.

"What'd she say? Hey?" said the grandfather on the end. And they started all over again.

Three minutes later, approximately, things were fairly well straightened out and the meeting underway.

"It seems," said the center grandfather, "that the Terror, wanting this female that just interrupted your grandfather, here, got himself involved with a couple of different types of characters, who may or may not be real people, ended up coming back here with one of the types of characters, known as a Shorty, hot after him, and killing one of the other types of characters, known as a Fatty. Everybody agree to this?"

There was a stir in the forefront of the crown and Gulark-*ay* spoke up.

"If the grandfathers will allow a stranger to speak—"

"Go ahead," said the center grandfather. "You're the Fatty top man from Humrog, aren't you?"

"I am."

"You don't agree?" said the center grandfather.

"I just," said Gulark-*ay* in a voice that reminded John of heavy maple syrup being poured from a five-gallon can, "wished to point out to the grandfathers of Clan Hollows that the Fatty in question is not quite killed. The Terror apparently left him for dead;

but it seems now he will recover."

"Well, then, there's no blood feud involved there!" said the grandfather, sharply. "Why aren't we informed properly about these things?"

"I didn't know," said the chief axman.

"Speak when you're spoken to," said the center grandfather. He looked out over the crowd. "Where's the Terror? I don't see the Terror."

"He's waiting at Glen Hollow," said Boy Is She Built.

"Shut up," said the axman who had spoken to her before.

"Let her speak now," said the center grandfather. "Unless somebody else can tell us why the Terror's at Glen Hollow instead of here? I didn't think so. Go on, girl!"

"The Terror says the Clan can't force a man to dishonor himself. If he'd known the Half-Pint Posted, this Shorty here, had been after him, he wouldn't have moved a step after taking Greasy Face to avenge his honor against Little Bite—"

"Hold on!" said the center grandfather. "Hold on. Let's get things straightened out here. Who's Greasy Face?"

Boy Is She Built pointed down at Ty Lamorc, beside her.

"This Shorty female, here."

The crowd muttered among itself and craned its necks, looking over the shoulders of those in front of it to get a look at Ty.

"Female!" the grandfather next to him was shouting in the ear of the deaf grandfather on the end. "Shorty FE-*male!*"

"They come in pairs?" the deaf grandfather said, interestedly.

Boy Is She Built went on to explain. It was approximately the same story Joshua had given John originally, except that in Boy Is She Built's version she and the Terror were reported as invariably speaking in tones of great calm and reasonableness; while Shaking Knees, Joshua, and all others sneered, whined, bellowed, and generally used the nastiest voices they were capable of using, when they were quoted.

"That still doesn't explain," said the center grandfather when she was through, "why the Terror isn't here to speak for himself."

"He says it already looks as if he had been dodging a fight with Half-Pint. He's not going to have it look as if he was hiding behind the grandfathers. He's there waiting for the Shorty now, in Glen Hollow for all the world to see. And if the Shorty doesn't reach him, it isn't his fault!"

"Hmph!" said the center grandfather, thoughtfully. He conferred with the other grandfathers. "Hey? What say?" the deaf grandfather could be heard demanding at intervals. Finally, they all sat back on their bench and the center grandfather spoke out again.

"As far as the grandfathers of the Clan can see," he said, "there's no reason this shouldn't be a personal matter between The Terror and the Half-Pint, here—except for one thing."

He paused and cleared his throat. It was like banging a gavel for order. The crowd became the quietest it had so far become.

"The facts are these," he said. "The Terror has had his mug spilt by a Shorty who is a guest in Humrog." He glanced at Shaking Knees. "Right?"

"Right," replied Shaking Knees, inclining his head

as one gentleman of substance to another.

"To hit back, the Terror has tried to spill the mug of the guest Shorty by stealing away a member of the guest's household. That little Shorty female, there, Greasy Face."

Everybody looked at Ty.

"All right. Now, along comes a male Shorty— Half-Pint Posted here—having a claim on Greasy Face, and chases after the Terror to get his female back. Of course the Terror can't honorably just *give* the female back. And the grandfathers of your clan aren't such unfeeling old geezers—" he paused to glare at the audience— "even though you all seem to think so most of the time, that they'd require him to give her back. So why not let the Terror and the Half-Pint meet? Well, there's only one hitch."

The center grandfather leaned back, readjusting the creases in his large belly and looked right and left for approval. With nods and grunts, his fellow grandfathers gave it to him. Even the deaf grandfather seemed to be fully briefed and in favor as he nodded with one hand cupped about his ear.

"The hitch is this," said the center grandfather. "Now the rules and customs of real men are not set up at random. There is always a purpose behind them. And the purpose behind affairs of honor is to enable real men to live honorably and safely, one with another."

"*I* it's absolutely ridiculous!" muttered Boy Is She Built. "What *I* think, is—"

"Shut up!" said the axman.

"Therefore, it is not just the honors of two individuals at stake in such instances, but the whole structure of custom by which we live. In this instance, now, it may well be honorable for man to fight with man; but is it honorable for man to fight a Shorty—considering all that a Shorty is, in the way of size and different-ness? In short, if we let this Shorty fight the Terror it's the same thing as admitting he's as much a man as any real man among us. And is he? What kind of proof have we got that he deserves to be treated like one of us, like a real man?" The center grandfather paused and looked out over the crowd. "Anybody who has anything they want to say on this question can now speak up."

"Ahem!" said Shaking Knees.

"Mayor?" said the center grandfather. Shaking Knees rolled forward a couple of ponderous paces.

"Just thought I'd clear the record," he said. "I don't claim to be any expert on the Half-Pint here, or Greasy Face, or any other Shorty. But I just thought I'd mention," he rubbed his nose with one large-knuckled hand, "that Little Bite here is a guest in Humrog. And speaking as the Mayor of Humrog, I don't exactly guess that Humrog would be making a guest out of anyone who wasn't entitled to be treated as a real man." He smiled widely around the crowd. "Just thought I'd mention it to you Clan Hollows folk."

The grandfathers consulted.

"Well, now," said the center grandfather, after the huddle was over. "The way the grandfathers of Clan Hollows think is this. Everybody here knows the folks in Humrog, after all we do most of our trading there. And we know that Humrog folks generally know what they're talking about. So if the folks in Humrog are pretty generally sure that Little Bite, there, is the same thing as a real man, the grandfathers of Clan

Hollows and the folks of Clan Hollows are willing to go along with the way they think, as far as Little Blue is concerned."

"Thanks. Humrog thanks you," said Shaking Knees.

"Not at all. However," went on the center grandfather, "deciding Little Bite can be taken for a real man, is one thing. Deciding Half-Pint, just because he's a Shorty, too, is a real man as well is something else again. After all, Little Bite didn't come hunting the Terror for an affair of honor—" he broke off suddenly, and his voice took on the first tinge of politeness it had yet shown. "One Man?"

"If I might—" the great basso of One Man rumbled politely off to John's left; and John, turning his head and peering around the bulk of the Hill Bluffer, saw the giant Dilbian rising. "If I might just say a few words to the eminent grandfathers of this ancient clan."

"The honor's ours, One Man," the center grandfather assured him.

"Very good of you," said One Man. The whole assemblage had gone dead silent and One Man's scarcely-raised voice carried easily to all of them. "An old man like myself, now, who has lived long enough to be a grandfather in my own clan, if I had one, and was worthy, sees things perhaps a little differently from you younger people. It's enough for me nowadays to sit feebly in my corner, letting the fire warm my old bones, and ponder on the world as it goes by me."

"Now, One Man," said the center grandfather, "we all know you're nowhere near's feeble as all that."

"Well, thank you, thank you," said One Man, lifting an arm like a water main in acknowledgement and then letting it drop, as if its weight was too much for him. "I've got a few years left, perhaps. But it wasn't myself I was going to talk about. I was just going to mention something of how things look to me from my chimney corner. You know, as I watch the passing parade I can't help thinking how much things have changed from the old days. The old customs are falling into disuse."

"Never said a truer word!" muttered the deaf grandfather on the end of the bench. He now had both hands cupped behind both ears.

"Children no longer have the old respect for their parents."

"You can bet on that!" growled Shaking Knees, scowling at his daughter.

"Everywhere, the old way of doing things is being replaced by the new. Where this will lead us nobody knows. It may be that the new ways are better ways."

"So there!" said Boy Is She Built, tossing her nose up at her father.

"We cannot, at this moment, say. But certainly we seem stuck with a world now in which we are not alone, in which we must deal with Shorties and Fatties, and maybe other creatures, too. This leads me to a suggestion which in my own limited judgment I consider rather sound; but I hesitate to push it on the venerable grandfathers of this Clan, being only an outsider."

"We'd be glad to hear what One Man has to suggest," growled the center grandfather. "Wouldn't we?" He looked around and found the other grandfathers nodding approval.

"Well," said One Man, mildly, "why not let them

fight and make up your minds afterwards whether
Half-Pint deserves to be regarded as a man—depend-
ing on how he shows up in the fight? That way you
don't risk anything; and whichever way you decide,
you've got evidence to back you up. For after all, it
isn't size, or hair, or where he was born that makes a
man among us. It's how he behaves, isn't that correct?"

He paused. The grandfathers and the crowd as
well, including such diverse elements as Shaking
Knees and Boy Is She Built, muttered their approval.

"A lot of people have thought that it might make
somebody like the Terror look foolish, facing up to
someone as small as a Shorty. Something or someone
that small, they thought, couldn't possibly have a
hope of standing up to a toothless old grandmother
with a broken leg. But the Terror seems willing. And
if the Half-Pint seems willing, too, who knows? The
Half-Pint might even surprise us all and actually take
the Terror."

There was a roll of laughter from the crowd and
One Man sat down. The center grandfather shouted
at the chief axman; and the axman shouted for order.
When comparative silence was re-established, it was
found that Gulark-*ay* had taken several ponderous
steps toward the bench of the grandfathers.

"What's this?" said the center grandfather, as the
chief axman whispered in his ear. He consulted with
his fellow grandfathers.

"Very well," he said at last; and raised his voice to
the crowd. "Quiet out there! The Beer-Guts
Bouncer's got something to say and your grandfathers can't hear anything short of a thunderstorm
with you yelling around like that!"

The crowd noise dwindled to near silence.

"Speak up!" said the center grandfather to Gulark-*ay*.

"Well, now, I kind of hate to shove in like this," said Gulark-*ay* in robust tones very different from the voice he had used to John, that morning before in the forest. He hunched his fat shoulders and was suddenly and amazingly transformed from a sleek Buddha to an overweight, but clumsily forthright and honest-looking, lout; somewhat embarrassed by being the center of all attention. "I wouldn't want to mess in the business of Clan Hollows, here. And I sure wouldn't want to say anything against that fine suggestion One Man made just now. But fair's fair, I say. I guess I ought to tell you."

"Tell us what, Beer-Guts?" inquired the center grandfather.

"Well, now," said Gulark-*ay*, scuffing the earth with one sandal toe, and turning red in the face. "Nobody likes Little Bite better than I do, but it's a fact, he's getting old."

"Something wrong with that?" inquired the center grandfather, sharply.

"No—no," said Gulark-*ay*. "Nothing wrong with it at all. But you know, Little Bite doesn't say much; but I happen to know he's been wanting to leave his job here and get back to his home on that other world, for a long time."

"What," said the center grandfather, "has all that got to do with us?"

"Well, Little Bite, he wanted to go home. But his people back there, they wanted him to stay here. Well, some little time ago he figured maybe he better just mess things up here a little; and then his people back home would send someone else out to do the job right and he could quit. Well now," said Gulark-*ay,* "*I* don't blame him. A Shorty his age, with nothing but real people twice his size around him all the time, it's not the sort of thing that would bother me, myself. But I can see how something like that would be for someone his size—like asking a kid to go out and do a full day's work in the fields, same as a man. And, of course, around here he doesn't have his machines and gadgets to make life easier for him. So, as I say, I don't blame him; all the same I wouldn't have done what he did. Didn't seem right."

Gulark-*ay* stopped to mop his face with a corner of his robe.

"Sure is thirsty, standing out here talking like this," he said. "I could go for a drink."

He got a good laugh from the crowd. But the grandfathers did not join in.

"What do you mean—'done what he did?' What did Little Bite do?" demanded the center grandfather.

"Well, he just thought he'd kick up a little ruckus by mixing into the Terror's business. Then Terror— any real person would have figured on it, of course— took off with Greasy Face and it got a whole lot more serious than Little Bite had bargained for. So he had to call in the Half-Pint there. Well, now, the truth is, the Half-Pint never saw Greasy Face before in his little life. It's all a story about him wanting her back from the Terror, like a real man might."

The center grandfather turned. His eyes focused on Joshua Guy.

"Little Bite?" he said.

"I'm right here," said Joshua, standing up.

"Is what the Beer-Guts Bouncer telling us, the truth?"

Joshua brushed some pine needles from a fold in his jacket with a casual flick of his hand.

"With all due respect to the grandfathers of Clan Hollows, and the people of Clan Hollows," he said, "I am a guest in Humrog, and a representative of the Shorty people. Accordingly, to dignify the Beer-Guts Bouncer's accusation by taking any notice of it would be beneath my official dignity."

Joshua smiled winningly at the Clan Hollows grandfathers.

"Accordingly," he said, "I must refuse to discuss it."

And sat down.

CHAPTER 16

THERE was a moment's dead silence and then the closest thing to a collective gasp that John had ever heard uttered by Dilbians. Being the type of people they were, it was more grunt than gasp—rather the sort of sound that comes from a punch in the stomach.

Then, a knowing babble arose.

The grandfathers sat back on their bench, looking grim. The center grandfather consulted to his left and to his right. Then he addressed the assemblage.

"Quiet down!"

They quieted, eagerly listening.

"Beer-Guts," said the center grandfather, to Gulark-*ay*. "You said Half-Pint here never even knew about Greasy Face until Little Bite got in touch with him. Then maybe you can tell us just why he'd come chasing after her, wanting to fight the Terror."

"He didn't," said Gulark-*ay*.

"He what?"

"Half-Pint," said Gulark-*ay*, "never even knew he'd have to fight the Terror, maybe, to get Greasy back. Little Bite never let on that might happen. If he had, he'd never have got Half-Pint to go after her. You don't think any Shorty would seriously consider tangling bare-handed with—what was it One Man said?—even a toothless old grandmother. Half-Pint wouldn't have been willing at all." He threw a grin at John. "He's not willing now. Find out for yourself. Ask him."

"Hey—" said the Hill Bluffer, shooting suddenly to his feet.

"Sit down!" said the center grandfather.

"Are you giving the government mail orders?" roared the Bluffer.

"Yes, I'm giving the government mail orders!" snapped the center grandfather. "On Clan Hollows ground, in full Clan Hollows meeting, I'm giving the government mail orders. Sit down!"

The Bluffer, growling, sat down.

The grandfathers went into session together. They talked for a minute or two, then sat back. The center grandfather spoke out.

"Here's the decision of the grandfathers," he said. "With all respect to One Man and others, this whole business smells a little too fishy to your grandfathers. Accordingly, it's our ruling that Greasy Face be sent back with Little Bite, and Half-Pint along with them. No affair of honor to be allowed between the Terror and the Half—"

"NOW YOU LISTEN TO ME!" thundered the Hill Bluffer, rising like a stone from a catapult. "Clan Hollows or no Clan Hollows. Grandfather or no grandfathers. And if the Beer-Guts Bouncer doesn't like it, he knows where to find the government mail, any time. You think this Shorty here isn't willing to tangle with the Terror?"

"Sit down!" yelled the center grandfather.

"I won't sit down!" the Bluffer yelled back. "None of you know the Half-Pint. I do. *Not willing!* Listen, when a bunch of drunks at Brittle Rock tried to make him do tricks like a performing animal, he fooled them all and got away. Then Boy Is She Built tried to drop him over a cliff. Does he look dropped? On our way here the bridge at Knobby Gorge was rucked up out of our reach. He climbed up a straight cliff with nothing to hang on to, to get it down and let us over after the Terror."

The Bluffer swung around and flung out a pointing arm at the chief axman.

"And what happened when you and four of the boys tried to take us in just outside the valley here? Who wanted to help me clean up on the five of you? And who didn't have any doubts about the two of us being able to do it, either?" He glared at the chief axman. "Huh?"

He swung around back to John.

"How about it, Half-Pint?" he roared. "The hell with the Clan Hollows and their grandfathers! The hell with anybody but you and me and the Terror? You want to be delivered or not? Say the word!"

John heard the Bluffer, and the swelling roar of the crowd rising behind him. All this time he had been sitting with one thumb rubbing pensively back and forth along the top edge of his belt buckle, listening to what was being said, and thinking deeply. He had time to figure out what was behind most of what was happening; and when the Bluffer had leaped up just now and gone into his impassioned speech, it had rung a bell clear and strong inside John Tardy.

So when the Bluffer bawled his question, John had his answer ready. The words were still in the air when John was on his feet himself, and shouting.

"Show me this skulking Terror!" he shouted.

"Lead me to him! Who hides behind his grandfathers and his clan and won't stand and fight like a man!"

CHAPTER 17

THE words barely had time to pass John's lips before things began happening. He felt himself snatched from the ground and the whole scene whirled wildly about him as he found himself being carried like a sack of grain away from the amphitheater and the meeting, and toward the forest beyond the valley.

The Hill Bluffer had grabbed him in two large hands and was running with him toward the forest the way a football player runs with a football. A roar of voices surged up and beat behind them. Looking back over the Bluffer's boulder-like shoulder, John saw that the whole mass of people involved in the meeting of Clan Hollows was now at their heels.

The free air whistled past John's face. He was being jolted about with every jarring footfall of the Bluffer; but the landscape was reeling past them both at a rate that must be close to thirty miles an hour; and the crowd behind was not gaining on them. In fact, John hesitated to believe it, considering that the Bluffer was carrying John's extra one hundred and eighty-five pounds in such an awkward fashion, but as the forest wall drew near he was forced to, they were actually running away from their pursuers. Their lead got bigger with each stride of the Bluffer. John felt the glow of competition as he had felt it on the sports

field many times before. For the first time, a spark of
kinship glowed to life inside him for the Bluffer.

They might be worlds apart, biologically, thought
John, but by heaven they both had what it took to
outdo the next man when the chips were stacked and
wagered.

Abruptly, the shadow of the forest closed about
them. The Bluffer ran on a carpet of tree needles, eas-
ing back his pace to a steady lope. He lifted John,
pushing him back around to the saddle. John climbed
into the saddle and hung on. With John's weight
properly distributed, the Bluffer ran more easily.

The surf-sound of pursuit behind them began to be
muffled by the forest. Moreover it was dropping
further behind yet, and fading. The Bluffer ran down
the side of one small hollow, and coming up the other, dropped for the first time back into his usual stalk-
ing stride of a walking pace. When he reached the
crest of the further side, he ran again down the slope
to the next hollow. And so he continued, alternately
running and walking as the slope permitted.

"How far to the Terror?" asked John, during one
of these spells of walking.

"Glen Hollow," said the Bluffer, economically.
"Half a—" he gave the answer in terms of Dilbian
units. John worked it out in his head to come to just
about three miles more.

A little more than ten minutes later, they broke
through a small fringe of the birchlike trees to emerge
over the lip of a small, cuplike valley containing a
nearly treeless, grassy meadow split by a stream,
which in the valley's center spread out into a pool
some forty feet across at its widest and showing
enough dark blueness to its waters to indicate some-

thing more than ordinary depth.

By the side of those waters, waited the Streamside Terror.

John leaned forward and spoke quietly into that same ear of the Bluffer's that he had bitten an hour or so earlier, as the Bluffer started down the slope toward the meadow.

"Put me down," said John, "beside the deepest part of that pond."

The Bluffer grunted agreeably and continued his descent. He came down to a point by the wider part of the pool and stopped while he was still about thirty feet from the waiting Dilbian.

"Hello, postman," said the Terror.

"Hello, Streamside," grunted the Bluffer. "Mail for you here."

The Streamside Terror looked curiously past the Hill Bluffer's shoulders and met John's eye.

"That's the Half-Pint Posted, is it?" he said. "I thought he'd be bigger. So the old ones let you come?"

"Nope," said the Bluffer. "We just came on our own."

While the Terror had been peering at John, John had been closely examining the Terror. John had gotten a fair look at the Dilbian scrapper back while he was escaping from Tark-*ay,* but from some little distance. And for most of that time, the Terror had been in pretty constant motion. Now John had a chance to make sure of the picture he had carried away from the Hemnoid camp before.

Once more, John was struck by the fact that the Terror did not seem particularly large, for a Dilbian. The Bluffer was nearly a good head taller. And the

impressive mass of One Man would have made two of
the younger battler. Streamside was good sized for a
male, but nothing more than that. John noted, however, the unusually thick and bulky forearms, the
short neck and—more revealing perhaps than anything else—the particularly poised stance and balance
of the Dilbian.

It was as if the whole weight of the Terror's body
was so easily and lightly carried that the whole effort
of moving it into action could be ignored.

John threw one quick glance at the water alongside.
The bank seemed to drop directly off into deep water.
He slid down from the saddle and stepped around the
Dilbian postman, kicking off his boots and shrugging
out of his jacket as he did so. His hands went to his
belt buckle; and in the same moment, with no further
pause for amenities, the Streamside Terror charged.

John turned and dived deep into the pool.

He had expected the Terror to attack immediately.
He had even counted on it, reasoning that the Dilbian
was too much the professional fighter to take chances
with any opponent—even one as insignificant as a
red-headed Shorty. John had planned that the Terror
should follow him into the water.

But not that the Terror should follow so quickly.

Even as John shot for the dark depths of the pool,
he heard and felt the water-shock of the big body
plunging in after him; so close that it felt as if the
Terror's great nailed hands were clawing at John's
heels.

John stroked desperately for depth and distance.
He had a strategy of battle; but it all depended on a
certain amount of time and elbow room. He changed
direction underwater, shot off at an angle up to the

surface; and, flinging water from his eyes with a backward jerk of his head, looked around him.

The Terror, looking in the other direction, broke the surface fifteen feet away.

Rapidly, John dived again. Well underwater, he reached for his belt buckle, unsnapped it and pulled the belt from the loops of his trousers. In the process, he had come to the surface again. He broke water almost under the nose of the Terror; and was forced to dive again immediately with half a lungful of air and his bulky enemy close behind him.

Once more, in the space and dimness of underwater, he evaded the Dilbian; and this time he came up cleanly, a good ten feet from where the back of the Terror's big head broke the water. Turning, John stroked for distance and breathing room, the length of his belt still trailing from one fist like a dark stem of water-weed.

Confidence was beginning to warm in John as he dove again. He had had time, now, to prove an earlier guess that, effective as the Terror might be against other Dilbians in the water, his very size made him more slow and clumsy than a human in possibly anything but straight-away swimming. John had gambled on this being true—just as he had gambled on the fact that, true to his reputation, the Terror would pick a battleground alongside some stream or other. Now, John told himself, it was time to switch to the attack, choose the proper opening and make his move.

Turning about, John saw the Terror had spotted him and was churning the water in his direction. John filled his lungs and dived, as if to hide again. But underneath the surface he changed direction and swam directly toward his opponent. He saw the heavy legs and arms churning toward him overhead; and, as they passed in the water, he reached up, grabbed one flailing foot and pulled.

The Terror reacted with powerful suddenness. He checked; and dived. John, flung surfacewards by the heel he had caught, released it and dived also, so that he shot downwards, behind and above the back of the Dilbian. He saw the wide shoulders, the churning arms; and then, as the Terror—finding no quarry—turned upwards again toward the surface, John closed in.

He passed the thin length of his belt around the Terror's thick neck, wrapped it also around his own wrists and twisted the large loop tight.

At this the Terror, choking, should have headed toward the surface, giving John a chance to breathe. The Dilbian did. But there and then the combat departed from John's plan, entirely. John got the breath of air he had been expecting at this moment—the one breath he had counted on to give him an advantage over the strangling Terror. But then Streamside plunged down again, turning and twisting to get at the human who was riding his back and choking him. And finally, and after all, John came at last to understand what sort of an opponent he had volunteered to deal with.

It is always easy to be optimistic; and even easier to underrate an enemy. John, it spite of all the evidence, in spite of all his experiences of the last three days, had simply failed to realize how much greater the Terror's strength could be than his own. Physically, the Terror in sheer weight and muscle was a match for any two full-grown male Earthly gorillas. And, in addition to this, he had human intelligence and courage.

John clung like a fresh-water leech, streaming out in the wake of the Terror, as the Terror thrashed and twisted, trying to get a grip with his big fingers on the thin belt, sunk in the fur of his neck. While with the other nineteen-inch hand he beat backwards through the water, trying to knock John from his hold.

John was all but out of reach, stretched at arms-length by his grip on the belt. But now and again, the blind blows of the Terror's flailing hand brushed him. Only brushed him—awkwardly, and slowly, slowed by the water—but each impact tossed John about like a chip in a river current. He felt like a man rolling down a cliff side and being beaten all over by baseball bats at the same time.

His head rang. The water roared in his ear. He gulped for air and got half a mouthful of foam and water. His shoulder numbed to one blow and his ribs gave to another. His senses began to leave him; he thought—through what last bit of semiconsciousness that remained as the fog closed about his mind—that it was no longer a matter of proving his courage in facing the Terror. His very life now lay in the grip of his hands on the twisted belt. It was, in the end, kill or be killed. For it was very clear that if he did not manage to strangle the Terror before he, himself, was drowned or killed, the Terror would most surely do for him.

Choking and gasping, he swam back to blurred consciousness. His mouth and nose were bitter with the taste of water and he was no longer holding the belt. The edge of the bank loomed like a raft to the survivor of a sunken ship, before him. Instinctively, no longer thinking of the Terror, or anything but light and air, he scrabbled like a half-drowned animal at the muddy edge of earth. His arms were leaden and weak, too weak to lift him ashore. He felt hands helping him. He helped to pull himself onto slippery grass. The hands urged him a little farther. His knees felt ground beneath them.

He coughed water. He retched. The hands urged him a little farther; and finally, at last completely out on solid land, he collapsed.

He came around after a minute or two to find his head in someone's lap. He blinked upwards and a watery blur of color slowly resolved itself into the face of Ty Lamorc, taut and white above him. Tears were rolling down her cheeks.

"What—?" he croaked. He tried again. "What're you doing here?"

"Oh, shut up!" she said, crying harder than ever.

She began wiping his face with a piece of cloth nearly as wet as he was.

"No," he said. "I mean—what're *you* doing here?" He tried to sit up.

"Lie down," she said.

"No. I'm all right." He struggled up into a sitting position. He was still in Glen Hollow, he saw, groggily. And the place was aswarm with Dilbians. A short way down the bank a knot of them were clustered around something.

"What—?" he said, looking in that direction.

"Yep, it's the Terror, Half-Pint," said a familiar voice above him. He looked up to see the enormously looming figure of the Hill Bluffer. "He's still out and here you're kicking your heels and sitting up already. That makes it your fight. I'll go tell them." And he strode off toward the other group, where John could hear him announcing the winner in a loud and self-justified voice.

John blinked and looked over at Ty.

"What happened?" he asked her.

"They had to pull him out. You made it to shore on your own." She produced a disposable tissue from somewhere—John had almost forgotten such things existed during the last three days—wiped her eyes and blew her nose vigorously. "You were wonderful."

"Wonderful!" said John, still too groggy for subtlety. "I was out of my head to even think of it. Next time I'll try tangling with a commuter rocket, instead!" He felt his ribs, gently. "I getter get back to the embassy in Humrog and have a picture taken of this side."

"Oh! Are your ribs—"

"Maybe just bruised. Wow!" said John, coming on an especially tender spot.

"Oh!" Ty choked up again. "You might have been killed. And it's all my fault!"

"All *your* fault—" began John. The dapper, small figure of Joshua Guy loomed suddenly over him.

"How are you, my boy?" inquired Joshua. "Congratulations, by the way. Oh, you must let me explain—"

"Not now," said John. He clutched at the small man's wrist. "Help me up. Now," he said, turning to face Ty, who also had risen. "What do you mean, it was all your fault?"

"Well, it was!" she wailed, miserably, twisting the tissue to shreds. "It was my off—official recommendation. The Contacts Department sent me out here to survey the situation and recommend means for beating the Hemnoids to the establishment of primary relations with the Dilbians."

"What's that got to do with me?"

"Well, I—I recommended they send out a man who conformed as nearly as possible to the Dilbian pyschological profile and we worked out a Dilbian emotional situation so as to convince them we weren't the absolute little toylike creatures they thought we were—but people just like themselves. We needed to prove to them we're as good men as they are, aside from our technology, which they thought was sissy."

"Me?" said John. "Dilbian emotional profile?"

"But you are, you know. Extroverted, l-lusty—. They've got a very unusual culture here, they really have. They're really much more similar to us humans when we were in the pioneering stages of culture than they are to the Hemnoids. We had to prove it to them that we could be the kind of people they could treat with on a level. The truth is, they've got chips on their shoulders because we and the Hemnoids are more advanced. But they can't admit to themselves they're more primitive than we are because their culture—anyway," wound up Ty, seeing John was getting red in the face, "it would have been fine except for Boy Is She Built trying to throw you over that cliff. She was only supposed to take your wrist phone. And that altered the emotional constants of the sociological equations involved. And Gulark-*ay* almost got it all twisted to go his own way, and—"

"I see," interrupted John. "And why," he asked, very slowly and patiently, "wasn't *I* briefed on the fact that this was all a sort of sociological power politics bit?"

"Because," wept Ty, "we wanted you to react like the Dilbians in a natural, extroverted, un—unthinking way!"

"I see," said John, again. They were still standing

beside the pool. He picked her up—she was really qute light and slender—and threw her in. There was a shriek and a satisfying splash. The Dilbians nearby looked around interestedly. John turned and walked off.

"Of course, she didn't know you then," said Joshua, thoughtfully.

John snorted, Dilbian fashion. He walked on. But after half a dozen steps more he slowed down, turned, and went back.

"Here," he said, gruffly, extending his hand as she clung to the bank.

"Thag you," Ty said humbly, with her nose full of water. He hauled her out.

CHAPTER 18

"I HOPE," said Joshua Guy, "you still don't consider that I—"

"Not at all," said John. He, Ty Lamorc, and the little ambassador, once more freshly cleaned and dressed, were waiting at the small spaceport near Humrog for the shuttle ship to descend from the regular courier spacer and take John and Ty back to Earth to be debriefed by the Contacts Department, there. It was early morning of a sunny mountain day and a light cool breeze was slipping across the concrete apron of the spaceport and plucking at the cuffs of John's trousers. A few curious Dilbian faces could be seen looking out the wide observation window of the spaceport terminal building, whose white roof glittered in the early sunlight about forty yards off.

"I got suspicious," said John, "when Gulark-*ay* gave me that long story about you when he, and Tark-*ay* and Boy Is She Built had me prisoner there in the woods. It was a little to good to be true—too good for Gulark-*ay*, that is."

"Oh, by the way, I ran into him as I was coming out from Humrog, this morning," said Joshua. "He told me he was due shortly for rotation to a post back on Chakaa—the second of the Hemnoid home worlds. If you and Ty dropped by, be sure to look him up and he'd show you around."

"No thanks," said John, grimly.

"My dear boy!" said Joshua, in tones of mild shock. "You mustn't confuse what a person does in his official capacity with his character as a private citizen. Drop in on Chakaa as a tourist or on official business, and I'm sure you'd find Gulark-*ay* a superb host. In fact, take my advice and take him up on the invitation. I assure you, you'll enjoy yourselves immensely." He interrupted himself to glance over at the building. "That Dilbian who's going with you two should be here by now. But pardon me for interrupting you. You say you only suspected—?"

"The story was too good to be true," said John, again. "What cooked it, to my mind however, was Tark-*ay* conveniently setting out his knife and going to sleep so I could escape. He and Gulark-*ay* meant me to escape all along. Of course," added John, "I don't think Tark-*ay* expected the Terror to come hunting Boy Is She Built just about then, and jump him. How is Tark-*ay*, by the way?"

"Recovering," said Joshua.

"I'm glad to hear it," said John. "He wasn't the worst sort of character to bump into, and I sympathized with him, being stuck with Boy Is She Built. But as I was saying, Gulark-*ay* wanted me to get away. I was no use to him in pieces. He wanted me to stand up in front of the Clan Hollows meeting and admit to everybody I was scared spitless of fighting the Terror."

"Lucky for us you weren't," said Joshua. "Actually, Ty and I never intended matters to go so far."

"We estimated that the emotional value of your simply coming after me would have a good effect on

the Dilbian group opinion where humans were concerned," put in Ty. "We wouldn't have blamed you a
bit if you had let Joshua take the blame of Gulark-*ay*'s
story and let the grandfathers send us back without
a fight. We didn't expect that kind of courage."

"What do you mean—courage?" said John. "If I
hadn't thought of the belt trick, and at that, it was a
crazy fool stunt because I'd gotten so used to the Dilbians I'd forgotten how strong they could be. Don't
ask me to try it again." He thought of something,
suddenly. "The Terror never said anything about
being beaten by a weapon, like my belt?" Joshua
shook his head.

"He's got his own reason, perhaps," said Ty. "The
Dilbian personality—oh, look!"

John and Joshua looked and saw One Man approaching, enormous in the morning light.

"Is *he* the one going with us?" said John. But One
Man joined them before Joshua could answer.

"Greetings to you all," rumbled One Man.

"Greetings to you as well," replied Joshua. They
smiled at each other, it was rather like a mouse and an
orangutan exchanging the time of day.

"Uh—" said John to Ty, "how'd you get that
smudge on your nose?"

"Smudge?" said Ty. "Nose?" She effected some
feminine sleight of hand which caused a large compact to appear and open in her fingers. She peered
into the mirror inside its lid. "Where? I don't see it."

"On the side of your nose there," said John. "It
looks," he added, "sort of greasy. . . ."

"Greasy!" Ty Lamorc snapped the compact shut
indignantly and headed toward the terminal building.
"Just a minute—tell the shuttle to wait," she called

over her shoulder. The two human men and the single Dilbian one watched her go.

"Attractive girl," murmured Joshua.

"Is she?" inquired One Man.

"By our Shorty standards, very," replied Joshua. "Our young friend here, the Half-Pint—"

"Oh, well," said John, and cleared his throat meaningfully. He looked at One Man. "If I could have a word with you—"

"Excuse me," said Joshua; and discreetly wandered off toward the far fence of the port.

"I wanted to thank you," said John.

"Thank me?" rumbled One Man, in mild basso astonishment.

"For your help."

"Help? Why, Half-Pint," said One Man. "I can't take any credit for helping you. I'm too old to go engaging in help to anyone, and if I did, of course it would be one of my own people. I can't guess what you could be talking about."

"I think you know," said John.

"Not at all. Of course, now that you've given my people a clearer picture of what Shorties are like—. Nothing wins like a winner, you know," said One Man, pontifically. "In fact, I'm surprised it took you Shorties so long to realize that. As I said to you once before, who asked you all to come barging into our world, anyway?"

"Well—" said John, uncomfortably.

"And what made you think we all *had* to like you, and welcome you, and want to be like you? Why, if when you were a pup, some new kid had moved into your village; and he was half your size but had a lot of playthings you didn't have, but came up and tapped you on the shoulder and said from now on I'm going to be your leader, and we'll play *my* games, how would you have felt?"

He eyed John shrewdly out of his huge, hairy face.

"I see," said John, after a moment. "Then why *did* you help me?"

"I tell you I don't know what you're talking about," said One Man. "How could I help a Shorty, even if I wanted to?"

"Well, I'll tell you how," said John. "Back home where I come from, we've got a trick with something called a city directory. It's about this thick," John measured several inches between finger and thumb, "and it's about as much a job for one of us Shorties to tear it in half as it is for one of you Dilbians to break that stick of yours. So—"

"Well, now, I can believe it," broke in One Man in a judicious tone. "Directories, sticks of wood, or first class hill-and-alley scrappers; there's a trick, I imagine, to handle almost any one of them. Of course," said One Man, gazing off at the pure snow of the far mountain peaks, "nobody like you or I would stoop to using such tricks, even in a good cause."

There was a moment's dead silence between them.

"I guess," said John at last, "I'll never make a diplomat."

"No," said One Man, still gazing at the mountain peaks. "I don't believe you ever will, Half-Pint." He returned his gaze to John's face. "If you take my advice, you'll stick to your own line of Shorty work."

"I just thought," said John awkwardly, "since you were coming back to Earth with us—"

"I?" said One Man. "What an idea, Half-Pint! An old man like me, exposed to all those new-fangled contrivances and being taught to act like a Shorty so I could come back and tell people about it? Why, I'd be just no good at all at something like this."

"Not you?" John stared. "Then who—?"

"I thought you knew," said One Man; and looked past John toward the terminal building. "Look; here he comes now."

John turned and blinked. Coming toward them from the terminal and holding his pace down to accommodate his stride to that of Ty, who was walking alongside him, was none other than the Streamside Terror.

"But—" said John. "I thought he—"

"Appearances," said One Man, "are often deceiving. If you were somebody with brains, among us real people on this world here, and nothing much else but a good set of reflexes, what would *you* do? Particularly if you were ambitious? Unfortunately, our society is a physically-oriented one, where muscles win more attention than wisdom. Streamside is the very boy to visit your Shorty worlds and begin to set up connections. Temperamentally, I can admit to you now, I suppose, you Shorties are a lot more akin to us than those Fatties. But you know how it is," One Man paused and sighed, "close relatives squabble more often than strangers do."

The Terror and Ty were almost to them. There was only time for a private word or two more.

"I hope he isn't feeling a little touchy," said John. "With me, I mean. After our fight, and so forth."

"You mean they didn't tell you?" said One Man. "Why, that was one of the Terror's conditions before he agreed to go. You see, evidently you Shorties have high hopes of setting up Dilbian-Human teams—"

John looked at One Man in surprise. He had never heard a Dilbian refer to either his own people, or any others by the human names for them "—and after initial contact work has been done, the Terror wants to pioneer that field, as well."

John frowned.

"I don't understand," he said.

"Why, the Terror's condition was that he be trained in your field and you be drafted to work with him, of course," said One Man. Staring up at the big face in astonishment, John was overwhelmed to see it contort suddenly in what, he realized after a second, was a pretty fair Dilbian imitation of the human expression known as a wink.

"You see," said One Man. "After the little episode in the water at Glen Hollow, he thinks you're pretty well capable. With you, he feels *safe*."